ARGENTINE ROAD RACE

PHILIP HARKINS

ARGENTINE ROAD RACE

WILLIAM MORROW & COMPANY
New York, 1962

4020

ACKNOWLEDGMENTS

To Joe Middleton and John "Taco" Randle, two
young racing car *aficionados* from Argentina, who
supplied the technical information for this book—
muchisimas gracias.

Philip Harkins
La Jolla, California

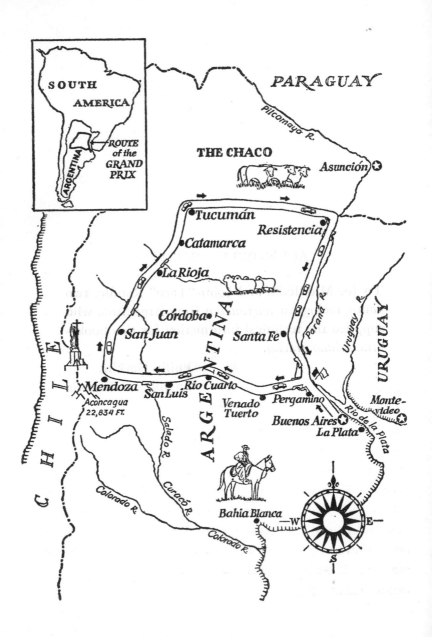

CHAPTER 1

ROSENDO FRAGA gunned the engine. It growled in a friendly way, and he shifted smoothly into second. As he stepped on the gas again, the three-liter, six-cylinder Talbot darted out on the wide, straight road famous for fast traffic. The highway was called the *Autopista* and it was in Buenos Aires, Argentina, far below the equator.

The growl grew louder. The needles on the speedometer and tachometer rose rapidly as Rosendo drew all the speed possible out of third gear, then shifted to high. Pleasantly exciting sounds began to swirl around Rosendo's ears. The wind whistled provocatively; raindrops, left on the hood by a recent shower, flew back and plopped against the windshield; the engine raised its voice to a roar; and small sounds of fear and admiration came from the girl strapped in the other bucket seat.

7

Rosendo Fraga had a theatrical disposition, and a fast car increased his histrionic tendencies. Today's spin in the Talbot was a small rehearsal for the greatest road race in the world, *El Gran Premio de Argentina,* just three weeks away. In the Grand Prix Rosendo would drive not the Talbot, but a special racing car.

"What kind, Rosendo?" asked Maria.

"A modified '46 Ford," said Rosendo, and he spoke with the tone of a man who has something up his sleeve.

Maria came in on cue. "A '46 Ford!" she cried.

Rosendo grinned, pleased with her reaction. "Yes," he said, "a '46 Ford. And that, Maria, is one of the reasons why the Grand Prix is the greatest road race in the world. All the drivers of these old American cars must use the original frame, the original body, and even the original block. We are not even allowed to rebore the cylinders. Think of it!"

"Amazing," said Maria. "But Rosendo—"

"Yes?" said Rosendo, arching his mustache.

"Why are only old American cars used?"

Rosendo's tone of voice became tolerantly didactic. "For three reasons, my dear Maria. One, because these cars are basically fast. Two, because they lend themselves admirably to modifications, and three, because they are sturdy. Bear in mind, Maria, that this fantastic race, starting right here in Buenos Aires, takes these cars and their drivers all over the country, over moun-

tains, through valleys, before bringing them back—
those that survive—to Buenos Aires."

"*Fantástico!*" said Maria.

Rosendo smiled. Maria had excellent reactions.
"Consider the cruising speed of my modified Ford,"
he said. "What would you guess it was, Maria?"

Maria looked at the speedometer of the Talbot.
"About the same as this—115 kilometers an hour?" In
Argentina speed and distance are measured in kilo-
meters, which are roughly three fifths of a mile.

"Two hundred," said Rosendo quietly.

"Two hundred?" cried Maria. "*Fantástico!*"

Rosendo was pleased. Once again the proper reaction had been achieved. He could proceed with the
performance. "And now," he said, "let me give you
a little taste of Grand Prix driving."

"Not too fast, please," said Maria.

Rosendo smiled. "Of course not," he said. Rosendo
was interested in skill as much as speed. Traffic on the
Autopista was light this sunny Argentine spring morning in November. There was plenty of room in which
to maneuver. Rosendo shifted to neutral and gunned
the engine. Now he shifted smoothly down to third,
flicked the wheel, and deftly took the Talbot past a
convertible. Stepping on the gas he spurted by another car, a coupé. It was just like a race and Rosendo
was winning. He shifted smoothly into high and soared
past another sports car.

The music from the engine rose to a crescendo. The

9

needles on the dashboard were metronomes measuring the accelerated rhythm in revolutions per minute and kilometers per hour. All the instruments were playing together in fast thrilling harmony—pistons, tappets, valves. Smiling, Rosendo opened his lips under his mustache to speak his most dramatic line—"And this, Maria, is how I shall drive in the Grand Prix."

Pinga-daping-ping-ping. Pock.

"*Diablos!*" cried Rosendo. Wrathfully he tromped the insubordinate gas pedal. It mushed. Rosendo Fraga's driving exhibition was ruined.

Years of experience as a race-car driver rushed to Rosendo's aid. He did not panic or twitch impulsively into rash action. He acted quickly, coolly, and smoothly. His left hand flipped up, alerting the following driver of a sudden turn to the right. Simultaneously his right hand took the wheel and maneuvered the Talbot out of the fast lane on the left while it still had steerage way. Having signaled his turn to the right and executed it, so that the nearest traffic behind him could pass on the left, Rosendo signaled again that he was stopping. In an emergency that called for cool and competent work at the wheel, Rosendo always gave a highly satisfactory performance.

Rosendo would now have to play the part of a pitman in the Grand Prix. He must lift up the hood, diagnose the trouble, and eliminate it. With a decisive click he unfastened his safety belt. With a less decisive grunt he heaved himself up out of his bucket seat.

He was too heavy—ten pounds overweight, perhaps fifteen—well, let's face it, twenty-five. He sighed as he extracted a clean rag from a leather kit.

Up went the hood, rolling raindrops to the street. Rosendo had come to the conclusion that the spark plugs, dampened by the shower, had begun to miss. That was it, all right, water on the plugs. Gingerly, so that he wouldn't soil the cuffs of his white shirt pinned together with huge cuff links, Rosendo wiped off the plugs. Then he squeezed back into his bucket seat and pressed the starter button. The motor whirled, the spark jumped, the gasoline exploded, and all six cylinders went into action with no trace of a *ping* or a *pock*.

"Wonderful!" cried Maria.

Rosendo smiled. "Nothing, really," he said with becoming modesty. Signaling, he swung out into the fast traffic of the *Autopista*. The Talbot's engine growled again as Rosendo smoothly and skillfully manipulated wheel, clutch, and accelerator.

Pinga-daping-ping-ping. Pock.

"*Caray!*" cried Maria.

"*Diablos!*" groaned Rosendo, as his right foot tromped the accelerator. Ignoring this chastisement the sports car quit, and Rosendo had to forget his anger and once again maneuver the Talbot out of fast traffic. As he did his anger ebbed and was replaced by bewilderment. What was wrong?

The car was now stopped safely, and Maria was saying, "So it wasn't the spark plugs after all?"

Rosendo bridled. He became haughty. "Perhaps yes, perhaps no," he said. "There is more to a plug than meets the eye. It might be the gap in the electrodes."

"Really?" she said.

"Exactly," snapped Rosendo. He pressed the starter button and the engine came to life again. How mysterious these engines could be! Rosendo wished his mechanic, Alfonso Salas, were present; on second thought he was glad Alfonso was absent. For Alfonso would certainly solve the problem quickly in his sour, sardonic way which implied that all drivers were idiots.

A *confitería*, a café, was conveniently near, and Maria bought a soft drink while Rosendo put on his second performance as pitman. From his tool kit he took a long socket wrench. Slowly his right hand lifted the first spark plug up to the light of the Argentine sun. Rosendo squinted at it like a jeweler examining a precious stone for flaws.

"Ah," he said significantly.

"What?" said Maria.

"The electrodes," said Rosendo. "See them, these two tiny wires? They're too far apart—too wide a gap." Gently he tapped the electrodes with a tool. "There," he said, "that should do it."

"Wonderful," said Maria.

"Nothing to it," said Rosendo, replacing the plug. He rested his wrench and reached for a cigarette from his silver case. Then he went back to work on the plugs. The work went forward rapidly. In a little while all the plugs, their gaps adjusted, were back in place. Rosendo now turned to Maria and said with an ingratiating tone in his voice, "Perhaps you would rather sit this ride out in the *confitería*."

"I was just thinking the same thing," said Maria.

"Fine," said Rosendo. "It will take only a few minutes."

"*Que le vaya bien!*" said Maria. "Good luck!"

Quickly now Rosendo guided the Talbot back onto the *Autopista*. He was running out of time. It was getting on toward the noon hour and the traffic on the *Autopista* was increasing. Soon it would be difficult to run at high speed, even for experts like Rosendo.

Maneuvering skillfully into a straight, uncluttered stretch, Rosendo shifted into high and stepped on the gas. The Talbot took off, the needles on the speedometer and the tachometer rising rapidly. As they reached the critical point Rosendo tensed at the wheel. He hunched over it, ears cocked, listening to the roar of the engine—

Pinga-daping-ping-ping. Pock.

"*Diablos!*" cried Rosendo.

Then came another jarring noise—the sound of a siren. Salt was about to be rubbed in Rosendo's wounds. He had not only failed as a mechanic, he was being arrested for speeding.

13

"Caray! Caramba!"

The representative of the law rode a motorcycle. He parked it and walked up to the Talbot, removing his goggles. A hand with a gauntlet reached out. "Your license," said the policeman.

Rosendo had it ready. He had also prepared himself psychologically, so that he would not lose his temper. Selling automobiles had developed an inherent shrewdness in his character. He only lost his temper when he knew he could get away with it. And he knew he couldn't get away with it in these circumstances. So he curbed his wrath and chewed his mustache silently.

"You realize that you were exceeding the speed limit?" asked the policeman.

"But by just a few kilometers per hour, *señor,*" said Rosendo. His tone was quiet, polite, humble, and apologetic. "In any case I am sorry."

"Sorry?" said the policeman, and cocked his head. "Sorry? That you would certainly be if you caused an accident."

"I have never been involved in an accident, *señor,*" said Rosendo smoothly, "except for one time and that was in the Grand Prix."

"The Grand Prix?" The policeman pricked up his ears. "You drive in the Grand Prix?"

"Yes, *señor,*" said Rosendo modestly.

"Rosendo Fraga." The policeman was reading the

name off the license. "Hmm. I seem to remember that name. How did you finish last year?"

"Not well," said Rosendo modestly. "Twenty-fifth."

"Hmm," said the policeman. "Twenty-fifth. Not bad, I would say. There were one hundred and forty-seven starters."

"One hundred and forty-eight, I believe," said Rosendo.

"One hundred and forty-eight," said the policeman. "And how many finished?"

"Seventy-four," said Rosendo.

"What a race!" said the policeman.

"The greatest road race in the world," said Rosendo with guarded enthusiasm.

"And right here in Argentina!" said the policeman proudly.

"No other country in the world has anything like it," crowed Rosendo.

The policeman handed back the license. "I am going to let you off with a warning," he said. "*Adios*, Rosendo Fraga, and good luck in the Grand Prix!"

"Many thanks, *señor*," said Rosendo.

They smiled, they waved, and they parted. Rosendo started up his sports car and drove back to the café. He was not feeling too bad. He had failed as a mechanic, but he had talked himself out of a traffic ticket. Besides, the girl, Maria, didn't have to know that he had failed. Instead of telling her how the engine had misfired at so many kilometers per hour,

15

he would take her to lunch and tell her how he had talked himself out of a ticket.

To Rosendo Fraga lunch was not a snatched sandwich and a chocolate malt. It was a long, leisurely meal that took about two hours to consume. Smacking his lips, Rosendo ordered one of his favorite dishes, polenta—corn meal cooked with cream and eggs and melted cheese.

"Not for me, thank you," said Maria. "I must watch my figure."

Rosendo chuckled and poured two glasses of wine. "And I, mine," he said. "Next week I go into training. I have to take off about ten pounds." He should, he knew, take off twenty-five, but there were only three weeks left before the race; there was a limit to the sacrifices one could make. He lifted his glass of wine. "To the greatest road race in the world," he said. They clinked their glasses.

After a few bites of the delicious polenta, Rosendo said, "Did you know, Maria, that *polenta* also means punch or power in a racing car? 'Give me more polenta'—that is what I am always saying to Alfonso Salas, my mechanic who drives with me."

"And Alfonso refuses?" said Maria.

Rosendo frowned. "He feels sorry for the engine. Ridiculous! The engine is not a human being—it does not have a nervous system. That is the trouble with Alfonso, really—his nervous system. He is too high-strung. When our speed gets up to 200 kilometers an hour he tries to bury himself in his bucket seat. As a mechanic working in a garage in Buenos Aires, Alfonso is excellent. But put him on the road in the Grand Prix—" Rosendo threw up his arms.

"It's too bad you can't have two mechanics," said Maria. "One to prepare the car for the race and the other to go along with you."

"Easier said than done," said Rosendo. But he considered Maria's suggestion while consuming another favorite Argentine dish, *bife a caballo* (eggs on horseback), two fried eggs on a steak. Why not have two mechanics? One could be Alfonso, who was good in Buenos Aires. The other could be younger, physically fit, and able to take the strain and stress of the race on the road. He would not have to be a master mechanic like Alfonso. He could be swift and skilled in the superficial—changing a tire or putting in a new set of plugs. The complicated work would have been done already.

When the long lunch was finished Rosendo dropped Maria at her apartment in the Flores section of Buenos Aires and set out on his own. He had decided to start a search for a junior mechanic before he went back to the automobile agency that he owned. His first stop was a service station on the *Rivadavia,* a long boulevard lined with acacia trees. Here a cheerful, healthy-looking youth sprang into action. Rosendo watched carefully as the youth quickly pumped in the gas and checked the tires and oil. The lad moved swiftly, surely, and cheerfully. How different from Alfonso Salas!

Rosendo had a bright idea. He could check out the youth's ability further by asking him to switch the two front tires. Casually Rosendo leaned out the window and made the request.

"*Sí, señor.*" The response was quick, pleasant, and polite. Rosendo glanced at the second hand of his wrist watch; he would time this promising lad.

Quickly the big jack rolled under the front axle. The young man pumped it up surely with brisk movements of his strong right arm. Now the tire iron pried off the hubcap cover; the lug wrench attacked the lugs. Off came the first lug. See that lug wrench spin! Rosendo was delighted.

But the second lug resisted. The lad had to grunt and heave. He had to give a louder grunt and a stronger heave. Without warning, the lug came loose and the young man staggered back and almost fell.

Rosendo frowned. Precious seconds in the pit were being lost.

"These lugs are stuck," the youth complained.

"Looks like it," said Rosendo, but his sympathy was feigned. Lugs were always stuck, except to a good pit-man.

The boy had a hard time getting the lugs off, and when this was done he did not drop them neatly into an inverted hubcab, but distributed them all over the place—in his pocket, on the mudguard. As a result he lost more seconds searching for some of them.

Rosendo groaned to himself. This would never do. Concealing his chagrin, he waited for the job to be done, paid his bill, and drove off down the *Rivadavia*.

As always, his dark eyes darted from one sight to another, taking in anything to do with automobiles—service stations, dealer agencies, and garages. The more you knew, the better, in the automobile business. He had heard of a new sports-car garage at the corner of the *Rivadavia* and the *Via de Flores*.

And there it was. It was owned and operated by an Argentine of Italian descent, Antonio Varela. It looked bright, neat, and promising. Rosendo decided to stop, size it up, and add another paragraph to his encyclopedia of general information. It could be more than a courtesy call, for his sports-car engine had been conking out at high speed. Perhaps Antonio Varela could spot the trouble. Rosendo drove in.

But where was Antonio Varela? This couldn't be Antonio, this slim, slight, lean-faced lad with an almost studious air. No, his name was Pedro; it was sewn on his coveralls.

Rosendo was rather disappointed, but he managed to make his greeting cordial. *"Buenas tardes,* Pedro."

"Good afternoon, *señor."* The voice was quiet, the accent just a little odd.

"Señor Varela, is he in?"

"No, *señor*. He is out on a job, but he will be back in half an hour."

"Ah," said Rosendo, "too bad I can't wait that long. But I shall leave my card."

Pedro read it. "Is there anything I can do for you, Señor Fraga?"

Rosendo hesitated. He had gone through one unfortunate experience with youth, and he didn't want another. And yet there was an air about this lad; there was something about the way he talked and the way he moved around that suggested skill and mechanical knowledge.

"Maybe," said Rosendo slowly. "This engine has been missing at fairly high speed on the *Autopista*." Rosendo's voice warmed to its subject and took on a tone of authority. "I checked the plugs and adjusted the gap on the electrodes."

"Did it make any difference?" The question was quiet.

Rosendo cleared his throat. "Ahem—no."

"Did you check the points, Señor Fraga?"

"Uh—no," said Rosendo. And added to himself, *Diablos!* Why didn't I think of the points? That girl, Maria, she distracted me.

Pedro was taking a feeler gauge out of his pocket. "Shall I check the points?" he said.

"Ahem—yes. Go right ahead."

The hood was up quickly, the cap was off the distributor nimbly, and the feeler gauge was measuring surely. The voice was quiet and calm. "You have a four-thousandths clearance, Señor Fraga. I think you need about a fifteen- or sixteen-thousandths with this kind of car. Would you check your manual, please?"

"Certainly." He reached for the glove compartment. The manual was there as it should be—page thirty-six for points—clearance, sixteen-thousandths. "Ahem. How careless of my last mechanic," said Rosendo.

"If you'll turn the engine over," Pedro was saying, "I shall also check the timing."

"The timing?" said Rosendo. "Naturally."

Pedro's timing light was flashing on the scale of degrees on the fly wheel. Then the young mechanic was back at the distributor, adjusting the breaker points and advancing the timing six degrees.

So the timing was off, too. "*Caramba!*" said Rosendo. "The last mechanic who checked this car must have been in a terrible hurry. Probably had a date with his girl friend." Rosendo laughed lightly.

Pedro merely smiled, and a thin smile at that. He was serious, this lad, yes indeed. And competent and quick and sure. Rosendo decided to proceed cautiously. He would find out more about this Pedro, using the technique that had worked successfully with customers —casual questions and sharp listening to the answers.

It did not take long for Rosendo to find out the essential facts. Pedro was nineteen years old. His last name was Thompson. His mother was Argentine and his father was a North American who worked for a meat-packing company. That accounted for the slight accent. He was a high-school graduate and was now attending night classes at a mechanical school in Flores. In high school he had played on the soccer team and had done some boxing; he still exercised when he could. His build was slight, but he moved well and was undoubtedly wiry. One more thing in his favor —he had done some car racing; not much, but some, in a small-time circuit called the *Meccanica Nacional*.

The tone of this fact-finding conversation was casual except for one instance. This took place when Rosendo mentioned why his sports car had been neglected recently—all of his mechanical energy was being directed toward the preparation of the car he would drive in the Grand Prix.

Having rolled this sentence glibly off his tongue, Rosendo waited for the reaction. He did not have long to wait. Pedro put down his wrench, looked up, and asked a question. He used the same quiet voice, but it now had a tone of respect. "You drive in the Grand Prix, Señor Fraga?"

Rosendo beamed. It was just the right reaction from a lad like Pedro. "Certainly," he said. "This will be my third race."

"That's wonderful," said Pedro. There was awe in his tone now. "How did you do last year?"

Rosendo chuckled modestly. "I'm not a grand champion yet," he said. "The first time I barely finished. Last year I came in twenty-fifth. The third time, this year"—the dark eyes flashed, the shoulders shrugged—"who knows? Number three is a peculiar number with me. Sometimes it means good luck, sometimes bad."

"I hope it means good luck," said Pedro earnestly.

"*Gracias*," said Rosendo. "My car is in good shape, I think. Have you ever worked on a Ford, Pedro?" The question was lightly asked.

"Of course," said Pedro quickly. "My own car is a Ford." He pointed. "Right over there."

Rosendo looked and saw a Ford V-8 about ten years old. His interest sharpened, but he kept its edge covered. "Modified, of course?"

"Up to a point," said Pedro. He smiled a small, shy smile. "Nothing like yours, of course, Señor Fraga. Yours would have a port-and-relieve job, things like that."

"Of course," said Rosendo, as if a port-and-relieve job were the most natural thing in the world.

"Wonderful," said Pedro. He returned to his work, finished it, and presented a bill with the same shy smile. "Perhaps you shouldn't pay, Señor Fraga, until you road-test your car."

"Nonsense!" said Rosendo grandly. "I have full confidence in your work." He paid the bill with a flourish.

"Try it out, *señor*," Pedro insisted. "And bring it back if it doesn't run right."

Rosendo slapped Pedro on the back. "You have my

23

card. Come by and have a look at the car I'll drive in the Grand Prix."

Pedro's eyes lit up. "I'd like to do that," he said.

"Any time," said Rosendo. He waved an arm in farewell and drove off in the Grand Prix manner, with deft turns of the wheel and a good deal of growling and snarling from the engine, heading for the wide, straight expanses of the *Autopista*. Pedro Thompson had made a favorable impression in the pit. But the real test of his skill would be right out here on the highway.

Smoothly shifting into third, Rosendo maneuvered the sports car into a clear stretch, shifted up to high, and stepped on the gas. Once again the needle on the speedometer climbed rapidly to the 100-kilometer mark and over. This was it. Rosendo's one-hand grip on the wheel became two-handed, at nine o'clock and three o'clock. His foot put more pressure on the gas pedal. When the needle on the speedometer reached 120, Rosendo held it there and listened tensely. He was not dramatizing this test. He was a Grand Prix driver who was worried about his temperamental mechanic and wondering about putting a young substitute in his place with the big race just three weeks away.

Right now that young replacement's mechanical work was being road-tested. And it was passing the test. The engine made many noises, but no *pings* and no *pocks*. It purred, it sang, and it roared. Rosendo was elated—the kid knew his stuff!

But not so fast. Pedro would make a good pitman? Possibly. But what about his potential as a copilot? Pedro said he had had "some" driving experience in the *Meccanica Nacional*. How much experience? Besides, road racing was quite different from driving on a closed track. The Grand Prix began in the heart of Buenos Aires and raced right through the city.

Alfonso Salas was just an average driver, but he could handle the car competently at 150 kilometers an hour. And there were certain times in the Grand Prix when 150 kilometers per hour was a satisfactory speed. Sometimes, in fact, when the drivers slowed down for cities, 100 kilometers per hour was fast enough. But at either of these speeds the driver had to have the right touch, that mysterious intangible quality, that feel of the foot on the gas pedal, that touch of the hands on the wheel and gearshift, that magic teamwork of the eye and brain measuring time and distance in split seconds. Pedro seemed to have it under the hood. Did he have it also at the wheel? Time alone would tell.

In the meantime, there was the final road test for the racing car with Rosendo at the wheel and Alfonso in the copilot's seat. That test was crowded with complications, tension, and temperament. Rosendo sighed.

He needed more time to resolve all these problems. The race was too close. And although he enjoyed its excitement and glamour, he shrank from its responsibilities. He liked looking forward to it, looking back on it, talking about it to his admiring friends. Dealing with the pressing problems it presented was unpleasant. Rosendo decided, therefore, not to deal with them for the present. He would sleep them off. His heavy, midday dinner had caught up with him. Before going back to the office, he would go home to his apartment and take a short nap. That would restore his energy and self-confidence.

Before falling asleep he made a good resolution, that he would cut down on rich food, wine and beer, and cigarettes. He would train, that's what he would do—starting tomorrow, or at least the next day, Saturday. No, there was a *fiesta* coming up. Well, Sunday would be a good day to start, or Monday at the latest. And with these noble, if rather indefinite resolutions, Rosendo Fraga slipped into his siesta.

CHAPTER 2

ROSENDO FRAGA met Pedro Thompson on a Thursday. In the late afternoon of the following Monday Pedro showed up at Rosendo's office to see the racing car.

Rosendo's greeting was only lukewarm. That very day he had started on his training program, cutting down on cigarettes, wine, and rich food. The comparative austerity had made him irritable. *"Buenas tardes,* Pedro," said Rosendo, and shook hands. But he did not rise from his desk. He tried to cover a yawn, failed, and with an effort said, "It is good to see you. You would like to look at the car I shall drive in the Grand Prix?"

"*Si,* Señor Fraga."

"It is in the garage of Alfonso Salas, my mechanic, about a mile from here. You have your car?"

"*Si, señor.*"

"Good." With an effort that he had often used to

make a sale, Rosendo smiled, heaved himself up from behind the desk, and said, "Let's go get a cup of coffee. Then I'll take you there myself."

Pedro protested. "But Señor Fraga, I don't want to inconvenience you."

Rosendo waved an arm. "It is nothing. It is the least I can do for a good mechanic who fixed up my sports car."

Rosendo's arm encircled Pedro's shoulders, and he guided him out of the office to a nearby café. Rosendo drank coffee, smoked a cigarette in his silver holder, and perked up. By the time they reached the garage he was in an expansive mood. Genially he introduced Pedro to Alfonso, a short, swarthy, taciturn man with gray hair at the temples, who was washing his grimy hands.

"I want to show this young man our racing car," said Rosendo.

"It is time to close," said Alfonso bluntly.

"Go ahead home, Alfonso," said Rosendo. "I'll lock up. After all," he said with a chuckle, "there are only two doors to lock."

"As long as they're locked," said Alfonso sourly.

"They will be," said Rosendo. "Go home and forget your worries."

"I have worries at home, too," said Alfonso. "You have forgotten my wife Angelina."

"An excellent cook," said Rosendo tactfully.

"And a sharp critic," said Alfonso, drying his hands

on a dirty towel. He ran a greasy comb through his thick, gray-flecked hair, pulled a cap down over it, slipped on a leather jacket, and departed with another warning to Rosendo about locking up.

Prowling around the garage while Rosendo and Alfonso talked, Pedro had found the racing car, half-concealed behind a partition in the rear. He was staring at the car with all the fascination and desire of a small and hungry child looking through a bakery window at a delectable display of cakes and cookies.

Rosendo smiled with satisfaction. "Well, what do you think of it?" he said. And without waiting for an answer, continued, "There's nothing magnificent about it, of course. It's just a '46 Ford coupé with an eight-cylinder engine. But the things that have been done to it!" Rosendo threw up his hands. "*Fantástico!*"

"I'm sure," said Pedro, in a low voice.

Rosendo reached for his silver cigarette case. He would give up beer, even wine, even polenta, but he needed an occasional cigarette, he told himself, especially in these times of tension. "Port-and-relieve job, naturally," he said. "I told you about that."

"Yes," said Pedro. "How about a special intake manifold?"

Rosendo fitted the cigarette into its holder. "Of course," he said.

"Racing cam?"

"Certainly." Rosendo pulled forth his silver lighter,

spun the wheel with his thumb, and studied the small, blue flame.

"How about the cylinders?" said Pedro. "Have they been rebored?"

Rosendo touched the flame to his cigarette, inhaled, tilted his head, and blew a shaft of smoke up at the grimy ceiling. His tone was slightly superior. "I'm afraid not," he said. "That's against the rules."

"What about fuel injection?" said Pedro.

Another shaft of smoke soared toward the ceiling. "Blowers are barred, too," said Rosendo. He was enjoying himself now and glad that he had made the effort to come along. It was heart-warming to see all this awe and interest on the part of a promising young man. And Rosendo was thankful that, like a good salesman, he had taken time to memorize all the selling points as well as the racing rules against rebored cylinders and superchargers.

"How about the carb?" said Pedro.

"Four barrels," said Rosendo, arching his eyebrows. He smiled. "Almost every inch of the car has something special. Look here." He opened the door. "See these hoses that run through the fire wall?"

Pedro peered in. "Yes."

"They go to the special oil pan. It's what we call a dry type. By means of a pump we can change the oil while racing. Saves a lot of time, eh?"

"It certainly would," said Pedro, impressed. "Do you use special oil?"

"All three weights," said Rosendo. "Twenty, thirty, forty. As you know, the race takes us all over the country—over snow-capped mountains, through hot, humid valleys. We have to be ready for all kinds of climate changes."

"Of course," said Pedro. "How about gas? How much can you carry?"

Rosendo exhaled smoke. "Seventy gallons," he said. Pedro whistled.

Rosendo continued, using his cigarette holder as a pointer. "This switch on the dashboard controls a second electric fuel pump in case the first one fails. In mountain driving an electric fuel pump proves its worth." Rosendo waved his cigarette holder and threw in a little quiz. "You know why, of course?"

The answer was quick and sure. "No fuel failure because of vapor lock."

Rosendo smiled. "Exactly," he said. The lad was bright and alert.

"How about brakes, Señor Fraga?"

"A good question," said Rosendo. "The brakes have wider linings and drums."

"More braking area," said Pedro.

"Exactly," said Rosendo, with just a touch of annoyance. "More braking area" was his line, not Pedro's.

"What about brake cylinders?" asked Pedro.

"Two for each wheel," said Rosendo. He gestured with his cigarette holder in the direction of the brake pedal. "And there are two master cylinders instead of just one."

"Extra shock absorbers, too?"

"Definitely," said Rosendo. "Two for each wheel. And extra leaves for the springs."

"Extra tires, too, of course," said Pedro.

"Not just tires, Pedro," Rosendo chided gently. "Five extra wheels. Some with heavy treads for mud and snow."

Pedro was shaking his head with admiration. "You and Señor Salas have thought of everything," he said.

"I think so," said Rosendo, a little annoyed that Señor Salas had suddenly popped back into the picture to take half the credit. "Everything has to be special for the Grand Prix, Pedro. The ordinary just won't work." He waved his cigarette holder at the front of the car. "Notice the wide core on the radiator. That's what is known as a tropical radiator. It keeps the engine cooler."

"An excellent idea," said Pedro.

"But that's not all there is to it," said Rosendo. "There is a special water pump, so that we can pump water up into the radiator while racing."

"Wonderful," said Pedro.

Rosendo smiled and said no more. Like a good salesman, he decided that the time had come to cut off the talk. Too many selling points tended to blur the customer's thinking. Deliberately Rosendo had omitted items that might seem routine, like roll bars and bucket seats. He had even left out the tail pipes, which were elevated up and over the mudguards to avoid water when the car splashed through mountain streams. Nor was there any need to say, "Well, Pedro, what do you think of the car?" That was obvious. Pedro was fascinated.

And this, thought Rosendo, is the way it should be left. Now he would speak an exit line and leave. He glanced at his wrist watch. "I'm afraid I must be going," he said. "I have a date."

"I hope I have not detained you, Señor Fraga," said Pedro.

"Not at all," said Rosendo, pleased by the youth's courtesy. There was no reason why a pitman shouldn't be polite. It certainly made for better relations with the driver. Yes, Pedro was an unusual lad. He knew a good deal about engines. He was alert, but not agressive. Apparently he was one of those boys who, at an early age, become fascinated by engines and subsequently steer clear of the more sophisticated amusements of the great city of Buenos Aires. Pedro wouldn't have to go into training; he was obviously already in it.

Then why not come right out with it and say, "Look here, Pedro, how would you like to be my copilot in the Grand Prix?" He could get a leave of absence from his job. His employer, Antonio Varela, would undoubtedly agree; it would bring prestige to his new shop; publicity stories in the papers: "Teen-age mechanic becomes pitman and copilot in the Grand Prix."

Rosendo weighed one factor against another and decided against an outright offer. The time was not yet ripe. Alfonso Salas was difficult, but not yet impossible, and he was a master mechanic and a veteran of the Grand Prix. As competent and promising as Pedro was, he would still be a novice with a big question mark beside his name. How would he react under the strain and stress, the fantastic wear and tear of the greatest road race in the world? To go into the race with that question unanswered would be to take a terrific chance. And Rosendo Fraga didn't feel like taking it.

One week later Rosendo was again driving his sports car to Alfonso's garage. But he was alone this time, and the hour was unusual—one o'clock in the morning on a cool spring night—the Argentine spring, which comes in the North American fall. There would be hardly any traffic on the *Autopista* at this hour, and the finest, widest road in Buenos Aires would offer the free-wheeling opportunities of a race track. The full polenta, or punch, of the racing car could be tested. Rosendo was looking forward to it with that mixture of excitement and apprehension that always precedes a race or road test.

Alfonso Salas had declared that he was finally satisfied with the condition of the racing car. Rosendo interpreted this to mean not only that the car was ready, but that Alfonso had decided to go along as its copilot. With only two weeks left before the race Rosendo had become increasingly averse to a radical change in the two-man team. It would definitely be better to answer the dip of the starter's flag with a grumpy but seasoned veteran than with a complaisant but untried novice. Rosendo was cheerful and congenial as he entered Alfonso's garage. In this road test he would handle Alfonso tactfully and courteously. Even if something went radically wrong Rosendo vowed he would not lose his temper and descend to name calling as he had on occasion in the past.

With this good resolution firmly in mind Rosendo listened patiently to Alfonso's gripes: he was tired, he did not like these middle-of-the-night road tests, his wife liked them even less, he was getting too old for this sort of adventure.

Rosendo listened with sympathy. He clapped his pitman on his shoulders, which were slightly rounded from ducking under a hood. "Absence makes the heart grow fonder, Alfonso. When you return from the Grand Prix after all the publicity, you will be a hero to Angelina. That's the way women are, Alfonso. They kick up a fuss when you leave on a great adventure, but they also fuss over you when you return, covered with glory."

Alfonso's answer was a grunt. Rosendo decided that enough palaver had been used on sales psychology. The time had come to get down to brass tacks. "I have the stop watch," said Rosendo.

Alfonso grunted.

Rosendo slid into the front seat, started up the engine, and played a few resounding chords on the gas pedal. "Beautiful!" he exclaimed.

Alfonso's answering grunt had a *gracias* in it.

Deftly Rosendo backed the car out of the garage onto the dark street. Alfonso locked up and joined the driver. Skillfully Rosendo nursed the car to the edge of the *Autopista*. He shifted down to neutral, gunned the engine, and in a deliberately casual tone said, "All ready?"

"*Sí*," said Alfonso, "if you insist."

"*Bueno*," said Rosendo. His heart was thumping against his ribs and his hands were moist, but his movements were fluid and precise as he let out the clutch. *Eeee.* Tires screamed and the car leaped forward. Smoothly, quickly, Rosendo shifted to second and asked for speed and pickup. *Vroom.* The engine roared its response in r.p.m.'s. Rosendo shifted to high, and the needle on the speedometer jumped to eighty, ninety, one hundred kilometers per hour.

"Now!" cried Rosendo.

Alfonso thumbed the lever on the stop watch and illuminated its dial with a small flashlight. "Nine-and-four-tenths seconds," he announced hoarsely.

"*Bueno!*" cried Rosendo, still manipulating clutch and gearshift. "That's a good pickup."

"*Gracias*," grunted Alfonso.

Rosendo was shifting to high, testing the car's cruising speed. The powerful engine roared, and the cool night air turned into an exciting whistle in Rosendo's ears. The needles on the speedometer and tachometer rose rapidly in r.p.m.'s and k.p.h. At 150 kilometers per hour Rosendo raced along the deserted *Autopista,* slowing down for the gradual curves, speeding up in the straightaways. The engine did everything it was asked for; the car handled perfectly.

Rosendo was delighted. When they reached the end of the *Autopista* he slowed down, relaxed, and complimented his mechanic. "Excellent, Alfonso, excellent."

For the first time Alfonso smiled. *"Gracias,"* he said. "We were turning 3900 r.p.m.'s at 150 k.p.h."

"Fine," said Rosendo, remembering that he had failed to watch the tachometer. But that was the mechanic's job. Alfonso was alert, ever mindful of the engine's performance. That was good. And so was the car's pickup and cruising speed. Alfonso had succeeded again. He was the logical choice for copilot in spite of his disposition and temperament.

Rosendo braked, swerved, and turned. He grinned at Alfonso, but the grin was forced. "Now for top speed, eh?"

"All right," said Alfonso. His tone was low and tense.

Rosendo's heart was thumping against his ribs, but his movements were just as smooth and skillful as ever. Here was the pickup, quick and good. Here was the cruising speed coming up again. The needles on the "tach" and the speedometer were rising rapidly,

150 k.p.h., 4900 r.p.m.'s. The engine was roaring and the wind was whistling, as the racing car barreled down the *Autopista.*

Rosendo became a man obsessed. He wanted every cubic inch of speed that the engine could produce, and he was determined to get it. The wild roar of the engine, the rush of the night air screaming in his ears were like wonderfully thrilling cheers urging him on to a supreme effort. The needle on the speedometer climbed to 200 k.p.h., trembled, and stopped. It would go no higher. Rosendo tightened his grip on the wheel, increased his pressure on the gas pedal. He looked as if he were trying to wrestle more speed out of the car. It was no use, the needle would go no higher; the car had reached its peak speed.

A look of disbelief came over Rosendo's volatile face. It gave way quickly to another expression as incredulity became disappointment, then irritation. *"Diablos!"* he cried. "Not enough polenta!" Irritably he eased the pressure on the accelerator.

As the speed slackened Alfonso continued to sit silently in his bucket seat. He stayed that way until Rosendo let all semblance of high speed drain out of the car, until it was rolling to a stop on a side street off the *Autopista.* Then Alfonso spoke. His voice was low and tense and it trembled a little. "What do you mean, not enough polenta?"

"Just what I said." Rosendo was making an effort to keep his irritation under control. "You know what

I mean, Alfonso. For racing out of Buenos Aires at the start of the race, 150 is all right. On certain country roads, 175 to 200 is all right. But there are also long, straight stretches that you should remember, Alfonso. It is on those straightaways that the winners are separated from the losers. Then and there is when we need that supreme speed—215, 220, 230."

"Look," said Alfonso, his voice still low and tense. "This car went from zero to one hundred in nine-and-four-tenths seconds from a standing start. What is wrong with that polenta?"

"Nothing," said Rosendo, "but—"

Alfonso interrupted. "It developed 4900 r.p.m.'s at 150 k.p.h. What is wrong with that polenta?"

"Nothing, but—"

Alfonso's voice rose. "But still you say my engine does not have enough polenta. Listen, Rosendo, do you realize what I have been through these last few months, sweating and straining over my engine?"

"Our engine," corrected Rosendo.

"My engine!" cried Alfonso. He snapped the buckle on his safety belt, got out of the car, stomped to the front, and lifted the hood. Then, taking a screwdriver out of the pocket in his coveralls, he proceeded in an indignant voice to give an illustrated lecture on the improvements he had made in this '46 Ford. As he made each point his voice rose in excitement and volume.

"And what have you been doing, Rosendo, while I

39

have been sweating and straining over these engine refinements?" Alfonso sneered. "You have been driving your girl friend around Buenos Aires in your sports car and boasting about how well you are going to do in the Grand Prix."

Rosendo rose up from his bucket seat and climbed out of the car. "I must remind you, Alfonso," he said carefully, "that I am the one who invests the money in this enterprise. I also happen to be the one who has the nerve and skill to push the car to those speeds which make victory possible in the Grand Prix."

"Push the car!" cried Alfonso. "Exactly. You push it, always! You never treat it like the sensitive thing that I have made it. You flog away at it like a stupid jockey whipping a tired thoroughbred. No wonder it fails in the stretch!"

This was too much for Rosendo. Advancing on Alfonso, he cried, "So that's why it failed tonight, eh? That's why it didn't have the polenta! That's what you think! Well, let me tell you what I think. I think it failed because of you—*bulonero!*"

Bulonero—boltmaker. The master mechanic gasped at the insult, then spat one back. "Charlatan!"

It was Rosendo's turn to gasp. Then he raised his fist. "No boltmaker is going to call me a fake," he shouted.

"And no charlatan is going to call me a *bulonero!*" cried Alfonso. "Charlatan!"

"*Bulonero!*"

Infuriated, Alfonso swung with the screw driver.

Rosendo side-stepped, dodged the blow, and swung with his fist. It landed. Alfonso stumbled back, tripped, and went down.

Immediately all the anger went out of Rosendo and was replaced by remorse. "Alfonso," he cried, "are you all right?"

Alfonso was sitting on the pavement, pressing his left cheek with his left hand. "You are not only a charlatan," he snarled, "you are a bully. You are twice my weight."

"I am sorry," said Rosendo sincerely.

"It is easy to be sorry," said Alfonso. "It is not easy to find another master mechanic. You and I are through. Our partnership is ended."

Rosendo pretended that he had not heard. He extended his hand. "Here," he said, "let me help you up."

"I don't need help," said Alfonso scornfully. Getting into the car, he settled silently into his bucket seat.

Rosendo slid behind the wheel. "Perhaps you should see a doctor," he said.

"For what?" sneered Alfonso. "This mosquito bite?"

Rosendo shrugged his shoulders. He could see that he couldn't win. The wise thing to do would be to keep quiet and wait for the storm to blow over. Worried, Rosendo drove Alfonso back to the garage. *"Buenas noches, amigo,"* said Rosendo, in another attempt at reconciliation.

"Adios," said Alfonso tersely.

Adios! It sounded ominously final to Rosendo. Returning to his apartment, he took two aspirins and went to bed. Worries engulfed him. He cursed himself for striking Alfonso. He berated himself—he must stick to his training program. He worried about the car—it didn't have enough polenta. It couldn't get up to that supreme speed, which would be needed on certain straightaways. Rosendo groaned. Then a suspicious thought insinuated itself. Had Alfonso Salas, master mechanic, deliberately overlooked some engineering refinement to keep the speed from being supreme? It was conceivable. Alfonso had become increasingly uneasy at high speeds. He seemed unhappy at 150 k.p.h., let alone 175 and 200. Perhaps he had no desire at all to compete in the Grand Prix. It was then perfectly possible that he would hold back mechanically.

Sabotage! That's what it was! In that case, Pedro Thompson would have to enter the picture. But he must be approached carefully—very carefully.

CHAPTER 3

EVER SINCE meeting Rosendo Fraga, Pedro Thompson had been thinking of the Grand Prix and the remote possibility of competing in it. His interest in the race was sharpened by the increased publicity the Grand Prix was receiving in Buenos Aires.

As Pedro's North American father had once told his son, Argentine interest in the Grand Prix reminded him of the American excitement over the World Series. There was a strong analogy between the two sporting events. Each occurred annually, lasted for more than a week, and stirred up nationwide excitement of fantastic intensity.

Pedro's father continued to be more interested in baseball than car racing, but he had assumed a tolerant attitude toward his son's interest in the faster sport. After some discussion about roll bars, safety belts, and crash helmets, he had allowed Pedro to compete in a limited amount of car racing. "I would rather have you drive fast legally than illegally," he had told his son. He had added another parental thought—that he appreciated discussing these adventures before Pedro got himself into them.

Bearing this in mind, Pedro brought up the subject of the Grand Prix.

His father's smile was incredulous, but sympathetic. "Don't tell me you're ready to drive in that?"

The smile and the tone of the question brought Pedro back to earth. Of course, he couldn't drive in the Grand Prix. It was ridiculous to think that he could. The realization was disappointing, though, for Pedro's secret ambition was to be a great driver—a glamorous, swashbuckling hero like, well, like Rosendo Fraga. Pedro had never confided this thought to anyone, not even his father. His family and his friends assumed that he was happy as he was, a quiet, modest, and unassuming mechanic. And Pedro lent authenticity to this impression by his actions and his ability to curtail his wishful thinking. Facing the facts, he knew that there were many years of experience between him and Rosendo Fraga, as well as, perhaps, a barrier of natural ability—the gift of inherited co-ordination, lightning reflexes. So Pedro swallowed his disappointment. He found a comforting thought, though; he might be able to compete much sooner in the Grand Prix, in say, two years, as a pitman rather than a driver.

Two years. It seemed like a lifetime this warm spring

morning in November as Pedro went to work. And there was nothing exciting in the shop on the *Rivadavia*, just routine jobs delegated by Antonio Varela, the jolly, chubby owner of the garage.

Pedro was still thinking of the Grand Prix when, just before the lunch hour, he heard a growl from a sports-car engine and a squeal of protest from tires. His heart beat faster when he looked up, for there was the Talbot and, behind its wheel, Rosendo Fraga.

"Buenos días, amigo!"

"Señor Fraga!" Pedro was delighted. Antonio Varela was cordial, but slightly confused. Señor Fraga quickly cleared up the confusion. He had come by to compliment Señor Varela for having in his employ such a fine young mechanic as Pedro Thompson, who had done such a quick, sure job on the Talbot.

Pedro's face turned red with embarrassment. He was not comfortable with such eloquent praise, but he had to admit that it had a warming effect.

Antonio Varela was also pleased. With a cordial greeting and a few hearty phrases, Rosendo had put everyone in a good humor. Antonio and Pedro were looking to him as if to a leader, and Rosendo did not disappoint them. *"Hola!"* he cried, with a glance at his wrist watch. "It is time for lunch. How about having it with me? There is a nice little restaurant not too far from here called La Mimosa. You know it, perhaps?"

Pedro knew it, but only by reputation. It was a hangout for race-car drivers, and fairly expensive. Usually Pedro ate his lunch out of a tin box.

Today, Señor Fraga insisted, they would all eat at La Mimosa. It was Antonio, the boss, who accepted the invitation for himself and his employee.

Hurriedly Pedro climbed out of his coveralls. Carefully he washed his hands and combed his hair, glancing in the small mirror over the grease-stained sink. Pitman. Grand Prix pitman perhaps. Did he look like one? What, after all, did one look like? A driver was supposed to be handsome, dashing, but there was no prototype for the pitman. Pedro glanced again at the image in the mirror, at the dark brown hair neatly parted, dark brown eyes, and ruddy complexion. He couldn't be called husky or handsome. But he was "not bad-looking"; there was a phrase he had heard at high school, where sports like soccer and boxing had given a supple wiriness to his slight build.

"Are you ready, Pedro?" It was Antonio, his voice impatient.

"Coming!" cried Pedro. He slipped on his leather jacket, gave one last glance in the mirror, and left the small washroom hurriedly. He had a vague, pleasantly uneasy feeling that this lunch at La Mimosa with Rosendo Fraga was going to lead somewhere. Where? He wasn't sure; he simply hoped.

La Mimosa was small and crowded, noisy and exciting. Clouds of smoke rose in wreaths to the low ceiling. Perspiring waiters, carrying trays of hot, fragrant food above their heads, squeezed past clusters of customers. There were few women in the place; La Mimosa was like a men's club. And Rosendo Fraga was obviously a member. The headwaiter greeted him cordially. Cries of welcome came from other tables.

Pedro's bright brown eyes were wide with excitement. There was Tomas Schmidt, well-known veteran of the Grand Prix, who spoke to Rosendo Fraga. There was Renaldo Gracciani; he, too, exchanged greetings. No doubt about it; Rosendo was not only a member of the club, he seemed to be a rather popular member.

And a good host. Summoning the waiter, Rosendo proceeded to ply his guests with food and drink. Pedro ate what he thought was the best food he had ever tasted, and listened, fascinated, to Rosendo Fraga. Señor Fraga was a performer, an entertainer. He told amusing stories about buying cars and selling them, he told exciting stories about the Grand Prix. He told how the cars were secretly tested at high speed on the *Autopista* in the dead of night. And then, quite casually, he asked Pedro if he would care to try out the car in a high-speed test, tonight perhaps?

Pedro had been fascinated by Señor Fraga's conversation. The challenging question, suddenly slipped into this conversation, struck him like a slap in the face. For a moment he was stunned.

Señor Fraga was watching, waiting. Eyes that had sparkled with entertainment now seemed sharp with challenge and bright with impatience.

47

With an effort Pedro restrained an impulse to cry, "Of course!" He forced himself to think the proposition over. Would he care to try out the racing car in a high-speed test? He could ask for nothing better. But on the *Autopista* in the dead of night, illegally? His father certainly wouldn't approve of that, and such an adventure without parental approval would mean sneaking out of the house and participating on the sly.

Señor Fraga, however, seemed to be taking an affirmative answer for granted. "I'll meet you at midnight," he was saying glibly. "You remember where Alfonso's garage is. We'll pick up the car there, get ourselves a cup of coffee—"

Pedro broke in. "I'm afraid I can't do it, Señor Fraga."

"Oh?" Señor Fraga braked, but only for a moment. Then he rolled on. "You can't tonight? A date, eh?" He winked and chuckled. "No matter. Tomorrow night will work out just as well."

"No, *señor*," said Pedro, looking straight at Señor Fraga and speaking quietly. "It is not that I have a date. It is that I would have to get permission from my father. And I am sure I couldn't get it."

A remarkable variety of expressions flashed across Rosendo's volatile face. There was a twinge of disbelief, a twitch of petulance, a twist of irritation. Señor Fraga started a sentence, "But you could . . ." and then stopped, apparently thinking better of it. He reached instead for his glass of wine, found a few

48

drops in it, drained them, and said, "Ah." Evidently that was all he could manage for the moment.

An embarrassing silence settled over the table. Antonio Varela did his part to end it. "I had strict parents myself," he said.

"My parents are not so strict," said Pedro quickly. "My father gave me permission to drive in the *Meccanica Nacional*. He said he would rather have me drive fast legally than illegally."

Rosendo Fraga cleared his throat. "Your father is right, of course." He turned. "Waiter! How about some coffee, Antonio? And you, Pedro? Good. That makes three. And the bill, please."

The coffee came. So did the bill. Señor Fraga paid it with a flourish and left a generous tip. As he drank his coffee he told another story. But the sparkle had gone out of his conversation. He seemed preoccupied. He glanced at his wrist watch, showed shock at the lateness of the hour, and announced that he had a business appointment. Would his guests excuse him? He was terribly sorry, but he must get back to the office. His guests could stay on, however, as long as they liked.

"We have to go, too," said Antonio. He smiled. "We have appointments also—with sports-car engines."

Rosendo Fraga returned to his office nursing his disappointment. He had expected Pedro to jump at the opportunity of driving a racing car. And what had the lad done? He had not only declined the exciting invitation, but had managed to put it in a rather bad light by bringing up the parent problem.

Diablos! thought Rosendo. Why, at my age, do I have to worry about parental approval? There was the rub, right there, in considering a teen-ager as a pitman. It all stemmed from that. Or did it? asked Rosendo's alter ego. How about that black eye you gave Alfonso Salas? The black eye he continued to wear resentfully, reminding his partner that their alliance had ended. And with the Grand Prix only two weeks away. *Caray!* And with the racing car still lacking sufficient polenta. *Caramba!*

As soon as possible these two essentials had to be found, polenta and pitman. That lad Pedro was the obvious answer. But in his naive, unsophisticated way he brought up irrelevant issues like parental approval. *Diablos!* A parent like that would probably not approve of his son's competing in the Grand Prix. And yet that same father who disapproved of illegal high speed allowed his son to compete in the *Meccanica Nacional*—where high speed was legal. Well, then, if that father pursued logical thinking, he should allow his son to compete in the Grand Prix as a pitman and an occasional copilot at the more moderate speeds.

Rosendo felt hopeful. He could arrange for a high-speed test on a closed track, the Autodrome. There would be nothing illegal about that. He could invite Pedro to come along with parental permission. Generously he could let Pedro take the wheel of the racing car for a couple of laps around the Autodrome. That would be a thrill for the lad—and a driving test for him too. Then, casually, he would ask Pedro's opinion about the car's polenta. Perhaps Pedro could pass both tests. Possibly he could not only drive the car well at high speed but, with his mechanical skill, seek out a solution to the polenta problem. Two enormous obstacles overcome with one jump!

Rosendo Fraga sighed. It was too much to hope for. He applied brakes to his enthusiasm. At the same time, with a few phone calls made with the touch of the successful salesman, he arranged for the high-speed test at the Autodrome.

"Pedro?" The voice belonged to Antonio Varela.

"*Si*, Antonio."

"Telephone. Señor Fraga."

"Señor Fraga!" Usually Pedro wiped off his grease-stained hands before answering the phone. Not this time. He grabbed it, grease and all. It slipped and banged against the desk on which it rested and sent a loud noise reverberating against Señor Fraga's eardrum. His voice, disembodied, squawked out of the dangling receiver, "What the devil's that?"

Pedro retrieved the receiver. "It is nothing, *señor*. The phone slipped." He was embarrassed to be awkward at such a time.

"Is it you, Pedro?"

"*Si, señor.*"

51

"Bueno. I'll come right to the point."

Pedro's heart had been beating fast. Now it began to thump. If Señor Fraga was coming right to the point instead of taking his usual circuitous route, something must definitely be up. It was. Señor Fraga had arranged for a high-speed test at the Autodrome, a closed track where high speed would be legal. Would Pedro care to come along?

Pedro almost dropped the phone again. A legal high-speed test at the Autodrome with a Grand Prix veteran! Would he care to come? *Caramba!* Would his father approve? Certainly, well, probably. Pedro said as much quickly.

"Bueno," said Señor Fraga, and gave the time and place of the rendezvous.

Pedro hung up, told Antonio the good news, and went back to work on a sports-car engine. With effort he kept at his work quietly, but not too calmly.

"Did you bring your crash helmet?"

Señor Fraga was asking the question of Pedro. They were at the garage of Alfonso Salas, who had gone for the day. Pedro, oblivious of all else, had been staring at the racing car. Recently painted a bright blue and white, it gleamed in the dim light of the garage.

Crash helmet. The term sobered Pedro's intoxicated mind. He had forgotten his helmet. It was embarrassing and irritating.

"No matter," Señor Fraga was saying. "I have a couple of extras in the back room. One should fit."

One did. It was not a bright blue and white like Señor Fraga's, but it fit well enough when Pedro tightened the chin strap.

"It will do," said Señor Fraga, and he smiled and tapped the helmet lightly with his finger tips, making a hollow sound on the hard plastic. "All ready? Seat belt fastened?"

"All set," said Pedro.

Casually Rosendo pushed the starter button. The motor whirred, the spark caught, and the modified engine of the Ford V-8 came to life with the roar of a lion rudely awakened from a nap. Nimbly Señor Fraga pumped the gas pedal like an organist summoning music. The majestic chords rose and swelled. Señor Fraga eased the pressure, let the sound fade, and spoke over it. "I have an interesting idea, Pedro. We'll detour to the Autodrome over the route the Grand Prix will take."

"A fine idea, Señor Fraga," said Pedro.

Rosendo continued. "It will be a sort of dry run for me. The better I know the route, the better I'll drive it."

"Of course, *señor*," said Pedro. He was delighted. They would drive over the Grand Prix route in the racing car. It would be almost like being in the race itself. Almost.

Señor Fraga handled the car smoothly, with speed

and skill. As they glided through the city traffic, heads turned. People stared and pointed. *"Mire!* Look!" A teen-ager whistled in admiration. Another called out, *"Gran Premio?"* Grand Prix?

Señor Fraga nodded and smiled and waved his cigarette holder in a chivalrous acknowledgment of the compliment. What a wonderful world! thought Pedro. Señor Fraga was an artist, a real performer, and such a smooth driver. And yet he led the traffic instead of being led by it. He picked the right openings, and exploited them quickly with deftly co-ordinated movements of gearshift and clutch, wheel and gas pedal. He drove rather fast, but did not exceed the speed limit. He observed all the laws and executed the necessary signals, but not with the jerky movements of an irritated driver unwillingly obeying harassing rules. An impressive performance. In no time at all they reached the Automobile Club, a handsome edifice on the wide *Avenida Alvear.*

"This is where the Grand Prix will start," announced Señor Fraga. "Right in front of the club."

Rosendo Fraga was smiling, but his tone was serious. It was as if he were already feeling the apprehension and responsibility that the event entailed.

Pedro felt some of it, too. To be here and in the racing car brought home to him again that fantastic fact about the great race—that it took place not on a track, but right here on the wide avenues of the city, and legally.

Señor Fraga waved his cigarette holder at the Automobile Club. "On the night the race starts there will be a ramp in front of the club. That ramp will hold one car at a time—one a minute. That's the interval between starters."

"How many cars will be competing this year, Señor Fraga?"

Señor Fraga smiled. "One hundred and fifty-three at the last count," he said.

"*Caramba,*" said Pedro quietly. What a scramble that would be! And Señor Fraga had finished twenty-fifth last year. There was nothing wrong with that.

"Let's start the dry run," the *señor* was saying. He had pulled over to one side of the wide *avenida* and stopped. Now, with gearshift in neutral, he gunned the engine. *Vroom.* He shifted to first, but kept the clutch pedal in as he glanced in the rear-vision mirror to see if the coast was clear. He smiled and spoke quietly. "The starter's flag is up . . . it dips."

Eeee. The scream came out of the tires as Rosendo Fraga peeled rubber. The racing car leaped forward, throwing Pedro back against his bucket seat. He stayed there as Señor Fraga poured on the power. *Vroom.* Señor Fraga gunned the engine again, shifted into high, and sent the racing car streaking down the *Avenida Alvear.*

Caray! cried Pedro to himself. *Qué pasa?* What's going on here? Does Señor Fraga think that the Grand Prix has actually started?

No. The roar of the engine was fading to a hum in high. The modified blue-and-white Ford was taking a prominent place in the stream of traffic, a spot that Señor Fraga had picked. He had simply shot the car into that spot with speed and skill. Now, his cigarette holder cocked at a jaunty angle under his mustache, Señor Rosendo Fraga guided the car down the *avenida* at the legal speed limit toward a concentration of streets called a rotunda.

In the center of this rotunda, which was like a hub of a wheel with streets as spokes, stood a monument. The traffic rushing around the rotunda reminded Pedro of the rapids in a river. Errant automobiles were rocks against which the racing car might crash and capsize. Beyond the rapids the rush calmed out in the continuation of the *Avenida Alvear*.

Señor Fraga shifted down and plunged the racing car into the rapids, swerving, braking, spurting. A teen-ager, driving a souped-up jalopy, zoomed menacingly out of a street on the right. Señor Fraga, anticipating the trouble, eased off the accelerator, braked lightly, and with a deft swing to the left avoided the collision.

Up front in the clear, nimbly avoiding another collision, Señor Fraga guided his car out of the rapids to the comparative calm of the *Avenida Alvear*. There he removed his cigarette holder and said, "On the night of the race, Pedro, the thing to avoid in that rotunda is the monument."

"*Sí, señor,*" said Pedro emphatically.

They sped on smoothly down the *Avenida Alvear.* Señor Fraga shifted down for a railroad underpass and a sharp curve to the right. He negotiated both nicely, shifted up into high, and followed the *avenida* as it ran parallel to the *Hipodromo* race track.

Shifting down again he swung left into the *Avenida Uriburu.* Here he swerved into a straight stretch, gunned the engine, shifted to high, and sped down the straightaway, driving fast but within the legal limit.

Pedro was all eyes and ears. He watched every practiced movement of the driver's hands—the right hand moving lightly and smoothly from gearshift to wheel, the left hand doing most of the steering in the straightaways, the left elbow resting casually on the car door. On the turns both hands held the wheel at three o'clock and nine o'clock, moving it deftly from left to right while the left foot worked the clutch and the right foot the gas pedal. It was all done so smoothly and casually that it seemed simple, but Pedro knew how much practice, training, and natural talent were behind those fluid movements.

"On the night of the race," said Rosendo, as they sped smoothly down the *Avenida Uriburu,* "this street will be a straightaway. The cars will hit 150 kilometers or better here."

"*Fantástico,*" said Pedro. No speeding tickets at 150 k.p.h.! In fact, the driver was rewarded for excessive

57

speed instead of being punished for it. For one night the rules were reversed.

Señor Fraga was shifting down for another turn. They drove toward the Autodrome, a closed track with long straightaways and exacting S turns. It was here that the Grand Prix would end in a matter of weeks. It was here, too, that Señor Rosendo Fraga's car would be tested—now.

"Let's put our crash helmets on." Señor Fraga's tone was casual, but Pedro thought the sentence was almost as exciting as the dip of a starter's flag.

They had driven onto the deserted Autodrome after Señor Fraga had exchanged greetings with the only attendant in sight. The track did not look formidable. It seemed asleep. No cheering crowds, no roaring engines disturbed its serenity. And yet, in its quiet way, it was impressive. Here the Grand Prix would end. Here high speed was legal.

What more could one ask? thought Pedro, as his fingers fumbled with the crash helmet's chin strap. The helmet was a little too big, but the chin strap helped it fit. Having fastened it securely, his fingers fumbled with his safety belt to make sure it was tight; he had no desire to be thrown out when Señor Fraga sent the racing car power-sliding through an S turn. But what was Señor Fraga saying?

"It's all yours."

Pedro was caught off balance. His tone showed his surprise. "You want me to go first?"

Señor Fraga was smiling as he left his bucket seat to change places. "You're the guest," he said.

Pedro was fumbling with his safety belt again. "Thank you, *señor*," he said aloud, but to himself he added, I'm not really ready. It would be better if Señor Fraga went first.

It would be better, perhaps, but it would be an admission of apprehension. And that Pedro would not admit except to himself. He moved over into the seat just vacated, the seat behind the wheel, the most important seat in the car. Here he was, all of a sudden, in charge of this powerhouse. It was up to him now to show that he could handle it.

The engine was purring. The gearshift was in neutral. The emergency brake was on. Pedro released it. Then he stepped on the gas, and the purr turned into an awesome roar that made his right foot tingle, a tingle that went up through him and down his arms to his moist fingers clutching the wheel.

He was trying desperately to remember all the things he should do, but his memory seemed to have deserted him. He was too nervous and he knew it. He decided to drive around the track once at a moderate speed to get the feel of the car and give himself time to calm down.

When he announced his intention, Señor Fraga nodded and said, "Good idea," as if he had been about to suggest it himself.

It was the power of the engine that perplexed Pedro.

59

He was delighted that it was there; it was exciting to hear it and feel it, but it was frightening too. It posed troublesome questions. If you use all that power, can you control the car? If you don't use it, will Señor Fraga think you're afraid?

The engine growled. It was a tiger, he thought, and he had it by the tail. It was roaring at him impatiently and now he would have to get on its back and ride it. He swallowed hard.

With a jerky motion Pedro pushed in the clutch and pulled the gearshift down to first. The time had come for motion—forward. Tentatively he let out the clutch, gently he stepped on the gas. It was as if he were squeezing the trigger on a rifle, anticipating a violent recoil.

The engine gave a loud, embarrassed cough as the car suddenly lunged forward and almost stalled. Quickly Pedro pushed in the clutch and gunned the engine. *Vroom.* There it was again with all its power. Unfortunately, it was not being used properly. In fact, it was hardly being used at all.

What was Señor Fraga thinking of this awkward exhibition? A glance to the right showed the *señor* sitting calmly in his seat. Whatever emotions he felt were hidden.

Gingerly Pedro shoved the gearshift into second and stepped on the gas again. This time he failed to let the clutch out soon enough. Consequently the engine mushed and more power was wasted. When the gears did grip, the car lunged forward again.

Pedro winced, but kept pressure on the gas pedal, letting the power of the engine pull it up and out of its awkward start. Now it began to run smoothly, strongly.

Pedro was awed; it was still in second! How fast would it go in this gear? Easily 100 k.p.h. The needle on the speedometer climbed to 125 and kept going. He shifted to high. He would go faster—150—faster!

But suddenly he caught sight of a sign by the side of the straightaway. Before it flashed by he read *300 meters*. That meant 300 meters to the S turn. So soon!

Immediately he eased off the gas pedal, braked, and shifted down clumsily. Another sign said *200 meters*, and he realized he was in second too soon. Then a third sign said *100 meters* and he found himself with control to spare. Quickly he stepped on the gas again, ashamed of the slow rate of speed. The car leaped forward and started to skid. He was going to spin out on his first turn! Alarmed, he eased the pressure and cornered with care. He realized that he should be skidding through this S turn in a power slide, steering with the accelerator.

Not this time. It was all too soon. He was not sufficiently familiar with the car. He was going to be sensible about this tryout even if it meant losing face. Sticking to this strategy he completed his tour of the

Autodrome, brought the car to a stop, and glanced to his right.

Was Señor Fraga disappointed by this caution? If so, he was concealing it behind a smile and a wave of his cigarette holder. "Well, Pedro, how did you like it?"

Pedro smiled back, but wanly. "It takes getting used to," he said.

"Of course," said Señor Fraga. "Now that you've made your trial run you can speed it up a bit, eh?"

Could he? Wasn't it contrary to his instincts? Pedro wondered. Was he doomed to being the steady, conservative type? He gunned the engine in neutral. It sounded friendlier. Shifting to first he engaged the clutch and stepped on the gas. He did not peel rubber, but the getaway was quick and smooth enough. So was the shift up to second. He was in high now, racing down the straightaway at a speed of 150 k.p.h. It felt good, it sounded good—the roar of the engine, the whistle of the wind. Here quickly was the 300-meter warning sign, the cutout point for cautious drivers. He did not use it this time, but kept the power on.

The second sign flashed by—*200 meters*. He braked and eased off the accelerator. Gunning the engine in neutral he shifted down to second, zoomed by the 100-meter sign, and drove rapidly into the S turn. He skidded a little but maintained his pace, steering smoothly. He cornered well, if carefully; coming out of the turn he stepped on the gas.

It was thrilling to feel that power, to know that he

had used it more efficiently. He shifted to high and kept pouring it on, glancing at the needles on the gauges to see the r.p.m.'s and the k.p.h.'s. The speedometer needle rose over 150 to 160, 165. It was a thrilling speed, but the car could obviously do better.

He did not ask it to. He eased the pressure, slowed down, and braked. Glancing to the right, he hoped for a look of approval on the volatile face. He did not find it. Was there, instead, a frown of disappointment? Pedro's heart sank. He felt that he had done as well as he could for the time and the place.

If there had been a frown it was gone, hidden behind a puff of smoke, a slightly superior smile, and a voice with a touch of condescension. "You got more out of it that time."

"*Sí, señor,*" said Pedro sadly. "I am sure that the car has a lot more power—"

"It does not have enough." The frown was clearly visible now.

"But it has a good deal," Pedro persisted. "Much more than the cars I drove in the *Meccanica Nacional.*"

"Of course," said Señor Fraga, with a touch of scorn. "But not enough for the Grand Prix, my boy. Here, let me show you."

Señor Fraga was up and out of his bucket seat. He seemed impatient now, and rather annoyed.

At me? thought Pedro. For my mediocre performance? Or at the car for its lack of polenta? Or at both?

Señor Fraga snuffed out his cigarette and put away

his holder. He swung his bulk into the seat hastily vacated by Pedro, who quickly fastened his seat belt. Just in time.

Eeee. The tires screeched. The car peeled rubber, hurtled forward, and barreled down the straightaway. Pedro was thrown back in his bucket seat, his oversized helmet jerked to one side, his breath snatched away. A quick glance to his left showed a different Señor Fraga.

Gone was the congenial boulevardier from Buenos Aires. Here was a different man—grim, determined, a man obsessed. There was going to be no trial run for Señor Fraga. He knew the track, and the car was going to get the works without any preliminaries. Swiftly but smoothly Señor Fraga put the car in high gear. In a matter of seconds the highest speed Pedro had reached in minutes was surpassed.

The cutout point Señor Fraga picked for his first corner was the 200-meter sign. When he shifted down for the turn there was no grinding of gears. The flick of the stick, the *vroom* of the engine in neutral spinning the gears into a more receptive speed, the double-clutching—all of this was fluid and slick, the work of an artist at the wheel.

Eeee. The tires were screaming in protest as Señor Fraga put the car into a deliberate skid and held it there, with delicate co-ordination of steering wheel and gas pedal. Here was a real "Grand Prix drift," a maneuver designed to take the racing car through the

S turn at the maximum speed and the minimum distance.

They were racing out of the corner, barreling up into the straightaway. Shifting swiftly from second to high, Señor Fraga hunched over the wheel, his right foot heavy on the gas pedal. The Grand Prix car was roaring; the needle on the speedometer was up over 200 and trembling as it tried to rise toward a supreme speed. Pedro was hanging on, his heart pounding, his eyes blurred, his ears tingling with the wild rush of wind.

Suddenly the 300-meter marker flashed in sight and Pedro tensed himself for another Grand Prix drift. But Señor Fraga was releasing the gas pedal from its heavy pressure. He was braking, scowling. He let out a cry of complaint. *"Diablos!* Not enough polenta!"

Not enough power? Pedro couldn't believe his tingling ears.

But Señor Fraga seemed drained of drive and determination. There was no thrilling Grand Prix drift in this S turn; he tooled through it listlessly.

They were back at the starting point now, and Señor Fraga was still scowling as he brought the car to a stop. Silently he took out his silver cigarette case, the holder, and his lighter. As he lit the cigarette, inhaled the smoke, and blew it out smoothly, he seemed to regain control. Casually Señor Fraga suggested a cup of coffee.

Pedro accepted the invitation gladly.

They sat in a *confiteria* sipping their coffee. Rosendo

Fraga was turning many thoughts over in his agile mind. Time was running out. The start of the great race was now only two weeks away. And two sticky problems persisted—the polenta and the pitman. *Diablos!* It was enough to drive a man out of his mind.

Casually, congenially, he brought up the problem of polenta. Of course, it would not seem like too great a problem to Pedro; a speed of 200 k.p.h. would seem sufficient. But there were certain stretches of highway in the Grand Prix where a car could reach and hold a speed of 240 k.p.h. "The car must have it." Rosendo tapped the table with his hand. *"It must have it."*

Rosendo made a suggestion. Perhaps Pedro would like to make a closer inspection of the car's engine? Perhaps he could come up with a suggestion or two? It was entirely possible that Alfonso Salas, in his absorption with complicated modifications, had overlooked a few simple things that might make a great deal of difference. And to himself, Rosendo added, it was also entirely possible that Alfonso Salas, who had become increasingly nervous at high speed, had deliberately overlooked a few useful modifications. Pedro could be an inspector, a friendly agent following the trail of a treacherous saboteur.

The lad's eyes were glistening. He was eager, delighted. *Bueno!* But *caray!* Here comes his conscience. You could almost see it coldly stalking his enthusiasm. Pedro was worried lest he intrude on the mechanical territory of Alfonso Salas.

Rosendo was almost indignant. Of course not. Alfonso Salas had resigned from the team—and that was putting it generously. It would have been more accurate to say that he had quit on the very eve of the race.

Had another copilot been signed up? Ahem. No, not yet. But several were being considered, yes, indeed. In fact, Rosendo was having lunch at La Mimosa the very next day to discuss the matter with another driver, a friendly rival named Juan Hunter, who had someone in mind.

Was there a flicker of disappointment in the lad's eager eyes? He had a hope, a dream. Yes, he was disappointed, but he was not downhearted. He was saying that he would be glad to look at the engine and give his opinion for what it was worth. If he could come up with some useful suggestions about the polenta, he would be a definite prospect. But he must not be told this. It would get his hopes up, and then they might have to be dashed.

There were other considerations. Pedro was just an adequate driver, or would be after a few more runs with the car on the Autodrome. To make up for that he should be a better than adequate pitman. This he could demonstrate by a few bright ideas about increasing the car's polenta.

That was that. They would meet tomorrow at the garage of Alfonso Salas. But not when that cantankerous individual was there. "Would 5:50 be agreeable to you, Pedro? *Bueno!*"

CHAPTER 4

PEDRO THOMPSON's emotions were mixed as he left the *confiteria*. He had not been happy about his performance at the Autodrome, and he could tell that Señor Fraga had been disappointed about it too.

It had therefore come as a delightful surprise to be called in as a consultant on the racing car's polenta. It would be presumptuous of him to second-guess the work of a mechanic like Alfonso Salas. Still, he had learned many new things at night school, as well as in the shop owned by Antonio Varela. He had always shown an aptitude for mechanical work, and now he had developed it into a real skill. It was entirely possible that a fine but temperamental mechanic like Señor Salas had, in his absorption with the complicated, overlooked the simple. It would not be the first time this had happened, as Pedro's instructors had pointed out.

Pedro was living in two worlds—the glamorous world of the Grand Prix, represented by Señor Fraga and his racing car, and the interesting job-by-job, class-by-class world provided by Antonio Varela and night-school instructors. It was in this second world that Pedro was able to think with complete calm and concentration. Tomorrow evening he would inspect the racing-car engine. Tonight and tomorrow he would make a mental list of the things in that engine, the simpler things, that might respond to treatment.

"Want me to start 'er up?" Rosendo Fraga was behind the wheel, Pedro under the hood. They were in the dim, cluttered garage owned by Alfonso Salas, who had already departed.

"Not yet, Señor Fraga."

"All right," said Rosendo. He was in a curious frame of mind. The situation was out of his control because of his lack of mechanical knowledge; he resented it and showed that resentment by his impatience. What was the lad doing, anyway? He seemed so slow. Pedro was checking the car's ignition, examining the plugs and the points. *Diablos,* thought Rosendo, we'll never get anywhere with these things. I could check them out myself.

Now wait a minute, Rosendo, said his alter ego. Curb your impatience. You know very well you couldn't do this work as well as Pedro. And you know why he's doing it. His only hope, as he said so modestly and quietly, was to find something simple that Alfonso had overlooked in his concentration on the big and the complicated.

Rosendo's worried mind went back to his lunch earlier in the day at La Mimosa. The purpose of the lunch had been to talk to Juan Hunter about a possible copilot and pitman. Unfortunately, the candidate concerned had just been signed up by another driver. *Diablos!* There was so little time left!

Hurry up, Pedro! Rosendo paced about nervously. He reached for another cigarette, restrained himself, and frowned. He had smoked his quota for the day. Was his abstinence improving his nerves? On the contrary, they seemed to be in worse shape, especially in times of crisis. And when wasn't there a crisis? *Caray!* This was one, certainly.

But one would never realize it by Pedro's cool and careful actions. What was the lad looking at now? The battery, of all things! *Diablos!* Next he'd be checking the air pressure in the tires. *Caramba!* They were all mad, these mechanics. It was unfortunate that engines were so complicated that they required the services of these maniacs. Now what was he doing? Probing into the four-barrel carburetor.

What could he do with that? It was a first-class carburetor. Get on with the job, lad! Come to a decision about something.

"Do you have a timing light, Señor Fraga?"

"Let me see." Rosendo stalled. Timing light. That

was the light that flashed on those marks on the flywheel. Of course. Aloud he said, "There must be one here someplace, Pedro."

But Pedro wasn't listening. He was peering into the gloomy darkness over Rosendo's shoulder. "Look out!" he cried.

Rosendo Fraga jumped and swung around. Then his eyes bulged and his mouth opened. For there in the shadowy darkness lurked a ghostly apparition—a sinister figure with a beard-stubbled face, a grease-stained cap, and a wrench held menacingly in its right hand. Alfonso Salas!

"*Caray!*" cried Rosendo, and sprang into a defensive stance, left fist up, right fist cocked.

Alfonso Salas snarled in a low, hoarse voice, "You sneaked in here to work on my car!"

"You are the one who sneaked in!" Rosendo cried. "And it's my car, not yours!"

This statement, reinforced by Rosendo's upraised fist, gave Alfonso pause. "All right," he said, "it's yours. Then get it and yourself and your young friend out of here!"

"Gladly," said Rosendo. He turned to Pedro, who was still staring in astonishment. "Come, Pedro, let's go."

"*Sí, señor,*" said Pedro, lowering the hood.

"*Adios,*" said Rosendo, as they drove out of the garage.

Alfonso simply glared.

So far, so good, thought Rosendo. They were coming out of a sticky situation unscathed. They could drive away in triumph.

But wait—they couldn't. They were now encumbered by three cars—Rosendo's Talbot, Pedro's old Ford, and the racing car. *Diablos!* One of the cars would have to be abandoned. But what was Pedro saying?

"Señor Fraga?"

"Yes, Pedro."

"I'll leave my Ford here and drive the racing car to your office. You follow me in the Talbot and bring me back here so that I can pick up my own car. Is that all right?"

Rosendo smiled. "A very sensible idea," he said. Clear, cool thinking. Simple, of course, but creditable. How many minds worked clearly and coolly under tension? This lad definitely had possibilities.

After the racing car was safely locked up for the night and Pedro had picked up his Ford, Rosendo suggested a cup of coffee. Pedro accepted the invitation, and they met at the *confitería*.

One thing was still uppermost in Rosendo's mind— the result of Pedro's inspection. He was extremely anxious to hear if Pedro had found anything wrong. But his salesman's psychology told him that it was still too soon to broach that vital subject. Rosendo reached for his cigarette case. He must have one more, quota or not. He deserved it; he had gone through an emotional wringer. These mechanics—one quiet, secretive; the other jealous, violent. *Diablos!*

Rosendo lit his cigarette, sipped his coffee, and said, "Too bad about that business at the garage. I'm afraid I put you on the spot, Pedro."

"I didn't mind," said Pedro. "I'm glad no one got hurt."

"So am I," said Rosendo. "Alfonso has quite a temper." He chuckled. "Now you can see how much tension the Grand Prix can create even before the race begins."

"Yes, indeed," said Pedro.

"People become unreasonable," said Rosendo. "Take Alfonso, for example. He walked out on me three weeks before the race, but he still talks of the car as if it were his!" Rosendo glanced at Pedro; what was the lad thinking?

"But all that fine work Señor Salas did on the engine," Pedro protested. "I can see why he would still consider it his car, in a way."

"Of course," conceded Rosendo quickly. And to himself he added, I must remember that this lad is a mechanic and looks at things from a mechanic's viewpoint. "Of course," he said again for emphasis. "I agree, Pedro."

Rosendo sighed. Pedro was fair—too fair! And he did not smoke or drink, and probably disapproved of those who did. It might be a nightmare to go on a Grand Prix with this paragon of virtue. And yet this con-

73

scientious young man could have the key to victory concealed in his coveralls; his cool and systematic inspection of the engine might have unlocked some of the secrets concerning its polenta. What Pedro had found out must be brought to light now. The time had come.

Rosendo blew a streamer of smoke over the table, leaned back in his chair, and in a philosophical tone said, "It's strange, isn't it?"

"What's strange, *señor?*" said Pedro.

Rosendo smiled. "That our unfortunate collision with Alfonso Salas could make us forget temporarily the whole purpose of our presence in his garage." Rosendo smiled again. He was well satisfied with that sentence.

"I didn't forget," said Pedro quietly.

Rosendo concealed a twitch. He was blunt, this lad. He reminded Rosendo of a customer who had once interrupted Rosendo's smooth sales talk for a car by saying, "I'll buy it."

Aloud Rosendo said, *"Bueno,* Pedro. In that case I'll come right to the point. Did you have time to see anything that might produce a little more polenta?"

The answer was quiet. *"Sí, señor."*

Sí! Rosendo sat up straight. He could no longer conceal his eagerness. "What, Pedro?" he said, making an effort to keep his voice from cracking the question like a whip.

74

"The jets in the carburetor," said Pedro. "They could be bigger."

Rosendo was leaning forward, his cigarette suspended. "Bigger jets in the carburetor," he said, as if wishing to engrave the phrase on his mind.

"The battery," said Pedro quietly. "It could be replaced by a magneto."

"By a magneto," said Rosendo, in a neutral tone. He did not want to seem surprised or ask why, for fear of revealing ignorance. He would wait, anxiously.

"At high speed," added Pedro, "a magneto is a better conductor for electrical current."

"Of course," said Rosendo. He was eager now, excited and optimistic. He could see the new polenta pouring into the car, the needle on the speedometer rising to new and wonderful heights.

"The timing, too, perhaps," Pedro was saying. "I might be able to advance it profitably. I was about to check that when Alfonso appeared."

"The timing, too," echoed Rosendo with enthusiasm. "Jets, timing, magneto." Rosendo repeated the words like an eager pupil parroting a teacher. Eagerly he asked, "The work on these three things, Pedro, could conceivably provide the polenta I want?"

"Quite conceivably," said Pedro quietly.

That was all Rosendo wanted to know. Pedro's theories seemed like the answer to Rosendo's prayers for more polenta. Carried away by his enthusiasm and his eagerness to have the days of indecision ended,

Rosendo cast caution to the winds. "Pedro, how would you like to be my copilot and pitman in the Grand Prix?"

The reaction was gratifying. Pedro registered surprise, awe, and delight. And then, quickly, control. He would, of course, have to get his father's permission.

Rosendo's frown vanished almost as quickly as it appeared. "Of course," he said. "But he will consent, won't he, Pedro?" he added hopefully. "I mean, after all, Pedro, he let you compete in the *Meccanica Nacional*. He let you make that test drive on the Autodrome. These things show that he is sympathetic—don't you agree?"

"Yes, I suppose so," said Pedro carefully.

Suppose, thought Rosendo impatiently. How cautious could one get? A sales talk was needed, one that could be passed on to Pedro's father. "Naturally, Pedro, you will be more of a pitman than a copilot. I shall do most of the driving and I have never, in all my racing, had a serious accident—never. All my risks are calculated, Pedro."

Pedro nodded.

"Of course, there is always an element of risk," Rosendo continued. He smiled. "But personally, I would rather take my chances in the Grand Prix, competing against experienced drivers, than I would around the rotunda on the *Avenida Alvear* in the late afternoon."

"*Sí*," said Pedro.

"Another thing," said Rosendo. "Going on the Grand Prix is an educational experience. You'll see a world you never dreamed existed—tense, exciting, courageous." Rosendo was in fine spirits. Now that the decision had finally been made, a great weight had been lifted from his shoulders. "Think of the country you'll see—Mendoza, the mountain city to the west, almost in Chile—Tucumán, to the north, the subtropical city that is called the Garden of the Republic."

Pedro was nodding, murmuring, *"Sí, señor."* His brown eyes glistened with excitement.

Carried away by his own high spirits and Pedro's enthusiastic reaction, Rosendo bubbled on. It was only when he returned alone to his apartment that he realized what he had done. Inspired by his own optimism, he had accepted Pedro's theories as if they were proven facts. They had yet to be tested. Suppose they were impractical? *Diablos! Caray! Caramba!*

Pedro was worried about getting his father's permission to take part in the Grand Prix. He was subsequently surprised by his father's reaction. Señor Thompson was neither angry nor antagonistic—he was startled.

"You?" he said. "You have been asked to participate in the Grand Prix?"

"As a pitman," said Pedro.

"Oh," said his father. "As a pitman. I see. And who is the driver?"

Pedro explained, and the next day Señor Thompson got in touch with Rosendo Fraga. Rosendo did a good job of selling the Grand Prix project, stressing points that he had previously expounded to Pedro. Señor Thompson gave Pedro his consent, and Pedro happily began his work on the racing car.

When he worked on the car he became completely absorbed, oblivious of everything but the engine. Señor Fraga, standing anxiously at his elbow, might as well be sitting in a *confitería* sipping coffee.

But when the work on the car was done, Pedro became very much aware of Señor Fraga's personality. This evening, two days after the encounter with Alfonso Salas, Señor Fraga did not seem to be his old familiar self. He and Pedro were driving out to the Autodrome to test the car for the new polenta, which Pedro hoped he had given it by his work on the jets, the timing, and the new magneto. Señor Fraga was silent.

Pedro thought he knew the reason why. Señor Fraga is worried about the work I did on the car. Will it or will it not produce the intensely desired polenta? I am worried, too. But I know that I have done my best. That is a satisfaction Señor Fraga does not have.

This tryout on the Autodrome was a complete contrast to the first one. This time Señor Fraga was not casually lighting a cigarette and saying with a smile, "It's all yours, Pedro." Silent, hunched grimly over the wheel, he did not so much as favor Pedro with a sidewise glance. He was concentrating completely on the job of driving, just as Pedro had concentrated on the mechanical work.

Quickly Pedro put on his crash helmet and made sure that his seat belt was secure.

Eeee. Señor Fraga peeled rubber. The car lunged forward, throwing Pedro back against his bucket seat. Swiftly they were in second, roaring down the straightaway.

Pedro was apprehensive, but he was also excited by the fast acceleration. He thought he could feel the pull of the new polenta, the full, free flow of the gas through the bigger jets in the carburetor.

The thrilling sounds that had become familiar rushed along with them—the roar of the engine and the whistle of the wind. Quickly, but smoothly, Señor Fraga shifted to high. They were racing down the straightaway toward the cutout signs in front of the corner. Carried away by the sounds and the excitement, Pedro thought, Surely this is the fastest speed ever attained by this car! I've produced the new polenta!

Proudly he glanced at the speedometer to confirm his hopes—and found them dashed instead. The needle of the speedometer stood at 200 kilometers per hour. It was a dazzling peak, but it had been reached before on this same track.

There was no new polenta here, thought Pedro glumly. His gloom was compounded by the appearance of the 300-meter marker. It was time to slow down.

I've failed, Pedro told himself. I have failed to provide the new power. But if that were true, why wasn't Señor Fraga complaining? Why was he continuing the test in his smooth, workmanlike way, easing off the accelerator, shifting to neutral, gunning the engine, shifting slickly down to second, and skidding through the S turn?

Why? There could be only one hopeful answer. Señor Fraga, as apprehensive as Pedro, had decided to warm up the new engine in the first straightaway and save the real showdown for the backstretch.

Eeee. The protest from the tires in the turn was more restrained than in the peeled-rubber start. Any teen-ager in a hot rod could peel rubber; it took a veteran to skid this skillfully through an S turn. A roar from the engine signified that Señor Fraga, who had been feathering the accelerator in the turn, had stepped on it. They were thundering into the straightaway. This is it, thought Pedro tensely. The work he had done would now be put to the big test.

Pedro hunched forward in his seat, as if to urge the car onward to the full use of its power. They raced up into high and hurtled down the straightaway. Now or never. The roar of the engine rose high as its every part strained under the relentless pressure put upon it by the grim driver at the wheel.

Pedro searched apprehensively for the 300-meter

marker. There was still a good distance to go—there was still time. Nervously he glanced at the needle on the speedometer. It was up over 200! It was rising rapidly to 210—215—220—230. It held there steadily in a delirium of noise and excitement. The new polenta was there!

Señor Fraga was crying *"Caray!"* but it was a cry of delight, not of despair. He eased off the accelerator and braked the car to a stop. His face, once tight and grim, was open and joyful.

"Caramba!" he cried, and with a quick turn and a sudden thrust of his right arm he whacked Pedro on the back. "You did it, Pedro, my boy, you did it! Now we'll show them, you and I!"

"Sí, Señor Fraga," said Pedro. He smiled. He, too, was relieved and delighted. There was just one small shadow reaching into the bright sunshine of this wonderful moment. It was a clear memory of Señor Fraga before the test—grim, silent, and tense—a complete contrast to this mood of unrestrained delight. Here, definitely, was a man of many moods. How many more? How many more were good and how many not so good? The Grand Prix, that great test of stamina and nerves, was sure to bring them all to the surface.

It was a sobering thought. But it did not endure. There was too much excitement in the air. The great race was now just a little more than a week away, and there was still much to be done.

CHAPTER 5

PEDRO THOMPSON had lived most of his life in Buenos Aires. He was a city boy, so absorbed by his work in the garage by day and trade school at night that he rarely thought of travel. There was no time for trips. He could remember packing a suitcase only once or twice in his life. Now he found himself packing not only a suitcase but a car, and he was bewildered by the number and variety of things that had to be taken.

Rosendo Fraga was not a mechanic, but his previous experience in the Grand Prix had provided him with a knowledge of equipment useful in emergencies.

They would take a couple of spare tires, Pedro suggested, pad of paper and pencil ready.

"We will take five spare wheels," said Señor Fraga emphatically.

"*Si, señor,*" said Pedro, and wrote it down—five spare

wheels. The coupé was going to be crowded; he could already see that.

As they went on to discuss the emergency equipment Pedro detected a certain trend in Señor Fraga's preparations. He seemed to be concerned chiefly with defects that could be caused by pressure driving—blowouts, fading brakes, slipping clutch.

The average car had one brake cylinder in each wheel, the racing car two. No matter. They would take extra cylinders for each wheel. Obviously Señor Fraga anticipated a great deal of braking. Señor Fraga shifted gears constantly. They would take an extra clutch.

Bewildered at first, Pedro caught on quickly, and started making his own contributions to the list. They should take extra points for the distributor, an extra condenser, an extra generator.

"*Sí*, Pedro." Señor Fraga smiled and nodded. He brought forth his cigarette case, lighter, and holder from his pockets. "I've smoked only three so far today," he said proudly. "Never been in better shape."

"*Sí, señor*," said Pedro. At first he had not thought too much of Señor Fraga's sacrifices. They had seemed rather small. To give up cigarettes, wine, creamed corn meal—was that really difficult? Now, as Pedro came to know Señor Fraga better, he altered his opinion. This would be quite a sacrifice for a man who was used to high living in the cosmopolitan capital. It would be difficult for him to go into training. Pedro had never really been out of it. He played soccer whenever he had free time, and even boxed a few rounds on occasion.

Señor Fraga was in high spirits these days. Pedro wanted to take extra fan belts and extra water hoses. "Good idea. Go right ahead, Pedro. My service department is at your command."

An extra half shaft, an extra universal joint? Señor Fraga considered these parts and nodded his head in solemn approval. Was he quite sure what they were for? It didn't matter.

Señor Fraga proposed the inclusion of two fire extinguishers. "And a complete first-aid kit," said Pedro. He followed this with the announcement that he had been taking a first-aid course.

"Diablos!" cried Señor Fraga. "What kind of catastrophes do you anticipate?"

"None, I hope," said Pedro. "But if I get a good kit I should know how to use it."

"I see," said Señor Fraga. "Well now, what about clothes? Sweaters and leather jackets will be needed for those cold mountain roads."

"Coveralls too," said Pedro.

"Of course," said Señor Fraga, "and a sports jacket and gray flannels. Don't forget, Pedro, there is time off, too, when the drivers and pitmen can wander around the plazas in delightful cities like Mendoza and Tucumán while the band plays and the pretty girls admire their heroes." Señor Fraga was smiling.

Pedro smiled back, but he wasn't too interested. He

didn't anticipate much time off. He would be working on the engine. Was it not true?

"Ah, yes," said Señor Fraga. His bright eyes twinkled and he twisted the ends of his mustache. "But 'all work and no play makes Juan a dull boy.' That is an old English expression that I learned from Juan Hunter."

Señor Fraga took a last drag from his cigarette and extinguished it. His tone now took on a touch of condescension—the veteran speaking to the novice. "Besides, Pedro, you must remember that when cars stop in cities like Mendoza and Tucumán they go into a supervised enclosure called a *parque cerrado*. When they are in this closed park, pitmen can work on them only at certain hours." Señor Fraga spoke these last two sentences with an air of triumph. Work was not only rather distasteful, it was forbidden.

"Oh," said Pedro. He was disappointed. Then he brightened. He had an idea. "In these periods of enforced idleness, Señor Fraga, we could have time for exercise?"

Señor Fraga frowned. *Exercise?* There was another distasteful word like *work*. Work was frequently prohibited by the *parque cerrado*. Then leave well enough alone; why spoil leisure with exercise?

But Pedro was persistent. "*Sí, señor,* exercise. We will need it after sitting cramped in the crowded car all day. *Señor,* listen—I shall bring along my soccer ball."

"Soccer ball?" said Señor Fraga in astonishment.

"I'm sorry, Pedro," he said, as he described the shape of the ball with a graceful gesture of his well-manicured hands, "but it would take up too much room." Señor Fraga's voice was serious, but his eyes were twinkling triumphantly. "Don't forget all those spare parts we're taking, Pedro. A soccer ball would displace any number of fan belts and water hoses."

"Not if I deflate it," said Pedro brightly.

"*Diablos,*" said Señor Fraga. He frowned. "All right, Pedro, you win. You can take your deflated soccer ball. Maybe it will stay that way," he murmured to himself.

"We'll have fun with that ball, Señor Fraga," Pedro bubbled on. "You know, nothing serious like a real game. Just running up and down a field, kicking it, passing it back and forth. You feel fine afterwards."

"I'm sure you do," said Señor Fraga absently. "You won't mind if I don't participate, Pedro? My left knee is fragile. An old polo injury. My pony fell on me— some time ago."

"I'm sorry to hear it, *señor,*" said Pedro. "At least it didn't leave a limp."

"No, I was lucky in that respect," said Rosendo. He glanced at his wrist watch. "*Caray!* I'm late! Maria will be annoyed."

It was Pedro's turn to frown. Was this date with Maria, whoever she was, more important than assembling the spare parts for the Grand Prix?

Señor Fraga noticed the frown. He placed a hand on Pedro's shoulder and smiled. "When you meet

Maria, Pedro, you will see why she makes me so anxious. Besides, you know more about these preparations than I do. It is obvious from the suggestions you have made. Help yourself to spare parts in the service department."

"Thank you, Señor Fraga," said Pedro. The *señor* was truly generous. There was no *peso*-pinching here. "Señor Fraga?"

"*Sí*, Pedro." Rosendo was on his way out, but he was trying to be patient.

"Would it be all right if I took the car out for another trial run at the Autodrome when I finish here?"

"Certainly, my boy."

"*Gracias, señor.*"

"*De nada*, Pedro. *Hasta luego*," and with a jaunty wave, Señor Fraga departed.

Pedro shook his head. Señor Fraga seemed to be neglecting his duties. He should be here supervising the packing. He should come along to the Autodrome and coach. But in a way Pedro was relieved. He liked to be on his own. It was fun to figure out what should be taken; to make up a list, check the items off, and help yourself to spare parts in the service department. Every item emphasized the wonderful event about to take place—the Grand Prix.

Thanks to Señor Fraga, he, Pedro, a teen-age novice, was going to take part in it. It was ungrateful of him to criticize the *señor's* social habits. From time to time Señor Fraga offered good advice. That was all that should be expected, Pedro told himself. He was getting along all right on his own. It was better for his own initiative and his sense of responsibility.

Moreover, he enjoyed it. He enjoyed driving the car to the Autodrome and having the kids point and call, "Look! There goes a Grand Prix car!" He enjoyed the test runs down the straightaways and through the S turns. He was getting used to the car, driving it better, faster, and more smoothly. He picked his cutout points later, nearer the turns. He was coming closer to that nice skiddy balance of speed without spin in the S turns. And he was coming out of the turns with a roar and a rush that saved time in the straightaways.

But he was not overconfident. He was truthful with himself. He was not, he knew, in Señor Fraga's class as a driver. Probably he never would be. But he would keep trying and improving, so that he could be useful as a copilot as well as a pitman.

Meanwhile, every spare part that he stowed in the rear of the coupé was not only catalogued, but charted. The list read as follows: one half shaft on floor, right front; one magneto, left rear, high. In the emergencies that were bound to come, Pedro could not only quickly confirm the presence of the spare part, but its location as well.

Rosendo Fraga, returning from the *confitería* or La Mimosa or the sales office, was impressed by the progress. "Bravo, Pedro!" he would exclaim with a pat on the back. "An admirable system." His eyes twinkled.

"Let us assume that the car is about to go into the *parque cerrado* at Mendoza. Ahead of you are several hours of enforced leisure or exercise. Where is your soccer ball?"

Pedro smiled as he consulted his list. "Soccer ball. Left rear, low, under spare magneto."

"*Bueno*," said Señor Fraga. "Deflated, of course?"

"*Sí, señor*," said Pedro. "It makes good padding that way."

"Good," said Señor Fraga, still smiling. Then he became serious. "Look, Pedro, I want you to save a space about two feet square for some special last-minute equipment."

"Certainly," said Pedro. Now what would this be? A gallon of special oil, perhaps, or some secret substance, which when added to gasoline would give it extra polenta.

Obediently Pedro saved the space for the special equipment. As he went on with his work the rear of the coupé began to look like a service department. It grew and grew, threatening to move up front and take over the bucket seats. To get behind the wheel Señor Fraga had to squeeze past an almost solid wall of accessories.

"*Caray!*" he cried the night before the race. "Pedro, you have really raided my stock. Is there anything left?"

"Oh, *sí, señor*," said Pedro. He smiled. "There is plenty left. We have everything we need now."

"I should say so," said Rosendo, with an apprehensive glance over his shoulder. "Did you save that space for my special equipment?"

"*Sí, señor,*" said Pedro. "What is it?"

"You'll see," said Señor Fraga, smiling.

"When, *señor?*" said Pedro.

"Tomorrow night," said Rosendo.

"Tomorrow night is when the race starts," said Pedro, and he could not keep out of his voice a tremor of excitement.

The day of the Grand Prix, Pedro's excitement grew hour by hour. He checked and rechecked his list of spare parts. He had arranged with Antonio Varela for his annual vacation to start on the same day as the Grand Prix began. Señor Varela let him off an hour early and sent him on his way with good luck and a present, a new wallet. Pedro went home to finish packing his suitcase and found a new one, another present. Pedro was more than touched; he was deeply affected, more so than he wanted to be.

He left home early, for he had to give the engine its last tune up—points, timing, and the four-barrel carburetor. Not to mention Señor Fraga's special equipment. That might take time to install.

Where *was* Señor Fraga? It was getting late. It was seven P.M., only five hours before the magic hour, midnight. Señor Fraga was at La Mimosa, undoubtedly, with some *compañero* or *señorita,* chatting, laughing, waving to friends and admirers. For tonight Señor

Fraga was a celebrity, a driver in the Grand Prix. He would be having the time of his life. Why shouldn't he be here like me, thought Pedro, sweating it out—going over the engine and checking the list of spare parts? Because it wasn't the kind of work Señor Fraga could do well. He would only get in the way. Pedro sighed, and went back to work. Minutes went by, an hour.

"*Hola*, Pedro!"

The anxious young pitman swung around. There was Señor Fraga standing in the doorway—happy, hearty, congenial—and carrying a large cardboard box. He advanced, bearing the box, and held it out to his pitman. "Here you are, Pedro, here is my special equipment. You have saved the space for it?"

"*Sí, señor*," said Pedro.

He accepted the box gingerly, opened it apprehensively, and stared in dumfounded disbelief at its contents—two big Thermos jugs, a large loaf of unsliced bread, and a roll of salami!

Señor Fraga was laughing at Pedro's consternation.

Pedro murmured, "It's a joke."

"In a way, yes," said Señor Fraga, "in a way, no. That is fuel, Pedro, fuel for the tired brain, that hot coffee in the Thermos jugs. The salami and bread are fuel, too, for the empty stomach. You realize, of course, that we won't have time to be stopping in restaurants."

"*Sí, señor*," said Pedro slowly, shaking his head. It

91

was a joke, but a useful one. It was foresighted of Señor Fraga, and typical. He, Pedro, was always thinking of the engine's appetite. Señor Fraga was concerned with human needs. Were they equally important? Perhaps. Pedro wasn't sure. He was confused, nervous. He had done everything he could think of, checked and rechecked. The start of the great race was now just a few hours away. He couldn't quite believe it, any more than he could believe that Señor Fraga's last-minute preparations concerned coffee and salami.

Señor Fraga was an extraordinary man. One never quite knew what to expect of him. Now he was calmly peeling the outer skin of the roll of salami with a penknife.

"You know, Pedro," he was saying, "there are people who actually eat this tough outer skin. They must have stomachs of iron. It would give me the most terrible indigestion."

"*Sí, señor,*" said Pedro. The strong smell of salami surged up and around Pedro's senses. They reeled. So did his thoughts. He wondered if he had forgotten anything for the car and marshaled his thoughts. Where was that check list? Here. Good. What about the *hoja de ruta,* the route sheet? Suppose he forgot that— *diablos!*

Gingerly he pushed his hand into the pocket of his leather jacket. Nervously his fingers closed on a sheet of paper and pulled it forth. He looked at it with a flash of relief. *Sí,* it was the *hoja de ruta,* the road map for the first lap of the Grand Prix, worked out in detail. All the directions were on it—the route out of Buenos Aires past the River Plata Soccer Club, the flat road to Pergamino, then on to Venado Tuerto and Rio Cuarto.

They should arrive at Rio Cuarto around eight in the morning. There would be a two-hour break there, then on to San Luis in the foothills of the Andes, then up to the mountain city of Mendoza, almost to Chile. *Fantástico!*

In just a few hours now they would be launched on this amazing adventure by the dip of the starter's flag. And what was the driver, Señor Fraga, doing—slicing salami! As he neatly stacked the sandwiches, Señor Fraga asked, "Do you have your *hoja de ruta,* Pedro?"

"*Sí, señor.*" Pedro produced it.

Señor Fraga studied the route sheet, murmuring the names—"Pergamino, Venado Tuerto, Rio Cuarto. I could almost drive it blindfolded," he said aloud. "The wise driver knows the route by heart. Look here, Pedro." Rosendo stabbed the *hoja de ruta* with his penknife. "Right here between Pergamino and Venado Tuerto there is a curve, which does not show its sharpness on the map. It will spin out many an unsuspecting driver tonight, Pedro, mark my words."

The penknife stabbed again at a railroad crossing farther along the route. "In the dark of night, Pedro, these railroad crossings look worse than they actually are. They intimidate some drivers. They reduce their speed too much and lose precious time. Will we, Pedro?"

Pedro was stowing the Thermos jugs in the space he had saved. He knew what the answer should be. "No, *señor*," he said. But he was sure that his answer lacked enthusiasm.

"Correct," said Señor Fraga. "We shall fly over those tracks, Pedro, like this." His right hand used a salami sandwich as an airstrip and took off into the evening air.

"*Bueno,*" said Pedro, but he was afraid his voice was weak.

"At approximately eight in the morning," said Señor Fraga, "we shall arrive at Rio Cuarto, a city in the center of an agricultural area. We cross the river on a bridge, right here, Pedro." The penknife stabbed again at the *hoja de ruta.*

"*Sí, señor,*" said Pedro.

"How did we approach the curve here?" The penknife moved back. "With caution and respect. The railroad tracks here? Like an airplane. *Bueno.* How shall we approach the bridge over the Rio Cuarto, Pedro?"

Pedro didn't answer. He knew Señor Fraga well enough by this time to know that the questions were rhetorical.

"With a combination, Pedro," said Señor Fraga, "a combination of caution and daring, a calculated risk." Señor Fraga gestured gracefully with his hands. "On

94

the gradual turn into the bridge I shall shift down and put the car into a Grand Prix drift. We shall skid nicely out over the river"—he chuckled—"on the bridge, of course."

"Of course," echoed Pedro hopefully.

"Here again," said Señor Fraga, "we have a mental obstacle in the minds of some drivers. Railroad crossings and bridges intimidate them as certain jumps intimidate steeplechasers. Not us, Pedro, eh?"

"No, *señor,*" said Pedro, as firmly as possible.

"*Bueno,*" said Señor Fraga. "We will do well together."

"*Sí, señor,*" said Pedro discreetly. He took the route sheet from Señor Fraga and carefully marked with a pencil the places Rosendo had stabbed with his penknife.

Señor Fraga slipped the stack of salami sandwiches into a paper bag. "You will notice, Pedro, that I made these sandwiches without butter. You will commend me, I trust, for keeping to my diet—no butter, no cream, no wine." He chuckled. "I have become a model of self-denial. Here, Pedro, stow these sandwiches with the Thermos jugs. You did save the space? *Bueno!* You are a good lad, Pedro. You are levelheaded. You plan well."

"*Gracias, señor,*" said Pedro. He stowed the bag of sandwiches securely beside the Thermos jugs and listened again as Señor Fraga talked of their rivals in the race—of Juan Hunter, Renaldo Gracciani, Rubin

Garcia, and Tomas Schmidt. All of them had finished ahead of Señor Fraga in last year's race, but then his car did not have half the polenta it had now. Moreover, he had made a few mistakes; he would be the first to admit it. Well, he would not make them again.

He was sure he could outdistance Juan Hunter and Rubin Garcia in this year's Grand Prix. But Renaldo Gracciani and Tomas Schmidt were strong rivals. However, Renaldo was not so good in the mountains; he got impatient with the narrow gravel roads and the endless hairpin curves. As for Tomas Schmidt—Señor Fraga sighed. Tomas was good anywhere. Just staying up there with him would automatically ensure a driver of a good finishing position. Tomas was a fine all-around driver. He was a pace setter; he kept bearing down. To keep up with him, to stay within range, and then to blaze by him on a straightaway—that was Señor Fraga's hope.

Pedro was listening as he puttered about the car making sure that everything was ready—gas, all seventy gallons of it, oil and water in the reserve tanks, the correct air pressure in the tires. Finally he said, *"Todo esta listo, señor."* All is ready.

"Vamos!" Let's go! Señor Fraga was eager, exhilarated. "Crash helmets!"

Señor Fraga had bought Pedro a new one, a perfect fit, painted blue and white to match the colors of the car.

They pulled on their helmets. Señor Fraga was

96

ebullient, but he did not let his enthusiasm influence his driving. He did not peel rubber. He drove carefully through the warm spring night as if to make sure that no accident, however slight, should mar his start in the Grand Prix.

As they approached the Automobile Club on the *Avenida Alvear,* Pedro sensed the excitement mounting. There was something electric in the air. Then he saw it in the cars parked along the side streets, the clusters of people converging on the club. He could hear it in the growing noise of the crowd, older people hurrying, young people running, pointing and calling to one another, "There's another Grand Prix car!"

"We're getting here none too soon," said Señor Fraga. He identified himself to a policeman, then to an official, and drove out onto the *Avenida Alvear,* which had been roped off. It was like coming out onto a blindingly floodlit stage from the obscurity of the darkened wings.

That impressive building, the Automobile Club, was ablaze with light. Flash bulbs popped like Roman candles, television lights glared. The collective conversation of the enormous crowd drummed on Pedro's ears like heavy rain on a thin roof. Piercing this background noise came the sharp call of the loud-speaker, rasping out announcements for the drivers.

Slowly Señor Fraga and Pedro drove through this organized pandemonium toward the cluster of officials.

"Rosendo!" A friendly call cut through the clamor.

Señor Fraga turned and waved to another driver in a red crash helmet, and said to Pedro, "That's Juan Hunter." Pedro looked and caught a glimpse of a fair face and a red-and-green car with the number 23 on it.

"Rosendo Fraga!" This time it was the rasp of the loud-speaker. "Rosendo Fraga! Please report to the starter's booth!"

"Coming, Mother," cried Rosendo with a laugh.

It was evident that Señor Fraga loved the lime-light. He was in the highest of spirits. Turning the car over to Pedro he bounced toward the starter's booth, shaking a hand here, slapping a back there. Judging by the reception he received one would say he had finished in the first ten instead of the first twenty-five. Still, to finish twenty-fifth wasn't bad in a field of a hundred and forty-eight starters. How many were there this year? One hundred and fifty-three!

With one leaving every minute it would take at least—Pedro calculated quickly—two hours and thirty-three minutes to get the Grand Prix going. *Caray!* This meant that the last car to start would not leave until twenty-seven minutes to three A.M. *Diablos!* To leave at approximately twenty-five minutes past midnight, by virtue of having finished twenty-fifth last year, was quite a privilege.

Juan Hunter in the red-and-green Number 23 was with the leaders. In front of Señor Hunter was another leader, Number 22, in a sleek black car with a white stripe. Number 21 was missing, but Number 20 was there, a strong-looking gray car with a yellow stripe. Number 19 was not yet in position, but Number 18 was in line—an impressive coupé painted purple and gold.

The more Pedro studied these cars, the gray, the black, and the purple and gold, the more they awed him. How much polenta was concealed under those glistening hoods? Plenty, undoubtedly; perhaps more, much more, than he and Alfonso Salas had worked into Number 25. Most of the cars in the starting line had their hoods raised and their pitmen were fussing over their engines. Pedro longed to do the same. He wished Señor Fraga would hurry back to take over the wheel and put the car in its official starting position. Then he, Pedro, could raise the hood and get under it, sheltering himself from all this glare and clamor.

Ah, there was Señor Fraga coming from the starter's booth at last. But he was meeting a friend, greeting him exuberantly, slapping him on the back. Must he always spend so much time in these greetings? He was on his way again now, finally.

"Rosendo!" The call was not only loud and clear, it was high-pitched and feminine. Pedro groaned. A *señorita*. Pedro scowled at her, but he had to admit to himself that she was pretty. He groaned again as he saw Señor Fraga take her arm and guide her toward the car. He was going to bring her over and introduce her—at a time like this!

This was no time for gabbing, greeting, or flirting.

No? Who said so? Pedro Thompson—just one half of the team, and the junior half at that. The senior half, Rosendo Fraga, obviously thought this was a time to enjoy, perhaps above all other times. Everything had led up to this time, the take-off. The stress and strain were yet to come. This was the *fiesta* before the fast—the glare of all the lights, the pop of the flash bulbs, the rasp of the loud-speaker, the noise of the admiring crowd, who could not yet tell if the driver was a champ or a chump. What mattered now was that he was a participant. Señor Fraga was one of the actors in this *fiesta,* and he was going to accept every bit of adulation that came his way.

Pedro calmed himself down, got up out of his seat, and bowed and shook hands with Señorita Maria Valdez. Maria was even prettier than she had looked from a distance, and although she was excited she did not seem too silly. She was very glad to meet Pedro, she said, but after a few polite phrases he retreated behind the engine's hood. As nice as Maria might be, he hoped she would go away quickly so that he and Señor Fraga could get down to business.

As if reading Pedro's thoughts, Maria lingered for just a moment. Then she held out her hand, and said, "*Adios,* Rosendo, *y buena suerte.*" Good-by and good luck.

Pedro looked, listened, and approved. That was the way to cut it off, cleanly and curtly. That girl had sense.

But sense did not satisfy Señor Fraga. He was taking

Maria's hand, pulling her to him, and kissing her. Pedro made a low noise of disapproval and hid under the hood. He vowed that he would stay there until the starter's checkered flag dipped.

The starter's flag was about to dip for Juan Hunter. The red-and-green car, Number 23, was up on the ramp two places ahead of Pedro and Rosendo. Twenty-two racing cars had already snarled off into the night one by one, minute by minute.

The clamor of the crowd had swelled to a deafening crescendo. The glare of the lights was as bright as the midnight sun. Pedro, sweating in the limelight, longed for the peace and obscurity of Antonio Varela's garage. His hands, fumbling with his seat belt, were moist with perspiration. His heart was threatening to break out of its cage of ribs. A dryness constricted his throat. Butterflies flitted about in his stomach.

"Buena suerte, Juan!"

The bellow from the next seat made Pedro jump. It was only Señor Fraga shouting above the din to his friend, Juan Hunter, wishing him good luck. Pedro wished Señor Fraga would be a little less exuberant. Pedro felt like a seasick voyager seated next to a hearty shipmate with a nauseating appetite.

Juan Hunter heard the shout. He turned and waved. Then he glanced up at the starter. The checkered flag was raised.

"Qué pasa?" cried Rosendo.

The starter's flag had dipped, but Car 23 was still on the ramp, motionless.

"*Caray!*" cried Señor Fraga. "He's stalled!"

Aruruh-ruruh-ruruh. Car 23's starter motor whined sadly. Derisive shouts came from the crowd. Pedro squirmed with sympathy for the poor pitman of Car 23. That unfortunate had unfastened his seat belt, jumped out, and hurried up under the hood. Juan Hunter, hunched over the wheel, was still stepping on the starter.

"*Que mala suerte!*" cried Señor Fraga. What bad luck. But the tone of his voice was not completely sympathetic. After all, Señor Hunter was a rival.

The crowd was jeering as attendants pushed Car 23 off the ramp while officials beckoned to Car 24.

"The race must go on," said Señor Fraga. "Poor Juan!"

And the poor pitman! Pedro was sweating. What happened to Car 23 might happen to Car 25. One never knew about these racing-car engines.

Rosendo, steering with one hand, was guiding the car to the foot of the ramp. His movements seemed more nonchalant than ever. He seemed determined to show everyone that he was completely unperturbed. Pedro squirmed in his seat, nervous thoughts whirling. Señor Fraga will stall it. Something will go wrong, and I won't be able to get it started again right away. The crowd will jeer, and we'll be pushed off the ramp in disgrace.

"*Hola,* Juan!" Another bellow from Señor Fraga twitched Pedro's taut nerves. Why couldn't he keep quiet and concentrate on keeping the engine running?

Señor Fraga, oblivious of his pitman's apprehension, was cupping his hands and shouting advice at Señor Hunter. "Did you check the clearance on the points?"

Juan Hunter's reply was terse. "We've already done it, Rosendo." It was evident from Señor Hunter's tone that he did not appreciate the advice.

Nor would I, thought Pedro. We should just go about our own business, keep the car from stalling, and get off to a good start.

Car 24 was blasting off the ramp with a defiant roar. Just one more minute now and Car 25 would be on its way. Just one more minute!

"Ten seconds," said the starter, looking at Car 25, and the warning quieted Señor Fraga instantly.

"Right," said Rosendo, and he shifted smoothly down to first. Then he disengaged the clutch and revved up the engine, stabbing at the accelerator with his right foot until the car rocked with restrained power like a strong, angry beast straining at a leash. The leash was the clutch, disengaged by Señor Fraga's left foot.

The starter's flag was raised, and Señor Fraga glanced up at it. "Three seconds," said the official, and he counted down. "*Tres—dos—uno!*"

Eeee. One of Señor Fraga's stabs at the accelerator

stayed there. At the same time his left foot snapped out the clutch. Señor Fraga had cut the leash. The rear wheels, spinning desperately, peeled rubber and sent Car 25 leaping from the ramp, pouncing on *Avenida Alvear* like a tiger springing on its prey.

CHAPTER 6

PEDRO was jolted back in his bucket seat, and a wild cheer from the huge crowd battered his ears. Faces flashing by in the crowd became a fantastic fresco. Car 25 *vroomed* through second to high, and all the sounds and sensations plunged Pedro into a trance. If he had not run over this route before with Señor Fraga, he would have been too dazed to see where they were going. But from time to time he recognized certain landmarks—certain landmarks like the monument in the rotunda.

Racing into the rotunda, Señor Fraga shifted down and put the car into a Grand Prix drift. They slid around the brightly illuminated traffic circle, with the great crowd on its perimeter wildly cheering them on. Pedro gripped the bucket seat, his hands wet with perspiration. Then he straightened up and stared. What was that cluster of people doing around the base of the monument? He caught a fleeting glimpse of a crumpled fender, a smashed radiator, and a white number 22 on something that was once sleek and was still black. Car 22 had crashed into the monument! A stab of alarm and anxiety pierced Pedro's trance. Had the crew of 22 survived?

There was no time to tell. Señor Fraga, glancing neither to right nor left, accelerated out of the Grand Prix drift, roared out of the rotunda, and raced down the *Avenida Alvear*. Gone was the hearty and congenial Rosendo of prerace time. He was more than serious now. He was grim, every inch a competitor. Car 23 had stalled? Too bad. Car 22 crashed? Bad luck. It was not going to bother Señor Fraga. He had a job to do. And he was determined to do it with all the skill and daring he could command.

Señor Fraga spurted along the brightly lit *Avenida Alvear* between a blur of cheering faces. Suddenly he shifted down to second with a *vroom* that echoed over the *Avenida*.

Why? Then Pedro saw with tear-blurred eyes the menacing steel supports of the railroad underpass. The car seemed to be heading right for them like a ship heading toward a shoal. Pedro's breath went out of him; he sucked in cool night air.

Eeee. The tires screamed in protest as Señor Fraga put the car into a power slide and skinned past the supports. The engine snarled as Señor Fraga applied more pressure on the gas pedal and zoomed them up and out of the underpass to the *avenida*. Recovering his breath and vision Pedro now recognized on the right the towering bulk of the *Hipodromo* race track.

Señor Fraga had made a race track out of the *Avenida Alvear*. Speeding past the hippodrome he shifted down and swerved to the left. A power slide and another shift with acceleration took them out of the turn and onto the *Avenida Uriburu*.

Pedro was beginning to come out of his trance. The way Señor Fraga had tooled through the rotunda and the railroad underpass had restored some of the pitman's shaken confidence. The first breath-taking dips in this wild roller-coaster ride had been taken; they had survived. There was a chance that they would continue to survive, for the man in charge of the car seemed to know what he was doing.

They were on the *Avenida Uriburu,* and Pedro realized that it provided a longer and better straightaway than the *Avenida Alvear*. Señor Fraga was obviously aware of it. The needle of the speedometer was rising to fantastic heights for a city street—150, 175, 200 kilometers per hour!

Pedro clutched his seat, his heart racing with the car. The blur of faces and the echo of the crowd's cheers added to the wild excitement. Señor Fraga responded to the cheers with heavier pressure on the accelerator. Desperately Pedro tried to remember how long this straightaway would last. Groping in his mind he recalled with alarm that the *Avenida Uriburu* ended in the fence of the firing range, dead ahead. They were doomed. They would smash through the fence, turn turtle, and crash on the range. They might as well be shot.

Pedro's alarming thoughts were still whirling when he felt a slackening of the car's speed. He saw the flick of the stick into neutral; he heard the gears rev up and whine down into second. Then came the familiar scream of protest from the tires. Pedro's mind seemed to go one way, his stomach another, and the rest of his body in a third direction. The force of inertia was pulling him straight toward the firing-range fence. Resisting it, he closed his eyes, leaned to the left, held on with all his might, and managed to go skidding around the corner with Señor Fraga in Car 25. They had made it. The fence was on their right instead of on their radiator.

But there was no time to relax and rejoice. The demon at the wheel was spurting up out of the power slide and propelling them forward parallel with the fence at a dazzling speed. It was a short stretch and Señor Fraga stayed in second for it. Then he braked, swerved to the right, and put the firing-range fence behind them.

Before Pedro's dazed memory could recall the next curve in the course, Car 25 was power-sliding through another rotunda, then barreling on down *Avenida Uriburu* at 200 kilometers per hour.

Desperately Pedro's bewildered mind struggled to

keep pace with the breath-taking speed of the car. Guiltily he remembered that one of the duties of the copilot was to keep the driver informed of the twists and turns of the route. But Pedro's hands were locked to the circular steel rod under the seat. They refused to abandon their grip to search for superfluous route sheets. Señor Fraga knew this part of the route by heart, but when they got outside the city limits the route sheet would have to be reached for and held ready.

The city limits? Weren't they already near them, so fast had been their pace? Señor Fraga was shifting down for another rotunda. This rotunda was different. It was at the foot of a slope. They were skidding down that slope now in a controlled skid. At the foot of the slope Pedro saw a fountain and a pool. With a stab of shock and alarm he saw something else—there was a racing car in the pool! He shouted, "There's a car in the pool!"

Señor Fraga acknowledged the news bulletin with a nod. He was steering with the accelerator, skidding nicely around the fountain. The tires were singing soprano.

Pedro was still staring. It was the gray car, Number 20. "It's Number 20!" he cried. "They're pushing it out!"

Señor Fraga nodded again. Car in the pool; Number 20; being pushed out. These news bulletins were accepted with astonishing matter-of-factness. They were interesting, they were pertinent; but they were not going to distract Señor Fraga from the job at hand. That job was to take Car 25 past all of these obstacles at a dazzling speed without cracking it up against a monument, driving it through a fence, or splashing it into a pool.

They roared up and out of the rotunda. The buildings grew smaller and darker, the cheering crowds thinned, the street lights dimmed, and the car's headlights came into their own. Pedro's bewildered thoughts began to pull themselves together. That rotunda with the fountain marked the city limits; they were now outside them. In a matter of minutes, rushing, roaring, skidding minutes, they were on a country road, dark and quiet and cool. Buenos Aires was behind them and they were racing toward the next city, Pergamino. The only noises were those they made themselves with the roar of the engine, the rush of the wind, and the scream of the tires in a turn.

It was a completely different atmosphere from the brilliantly illuminated streets of the city and the wildly cheering crowds. It helped Pedro begin to come to his senses. He forced himself into the realization that he was a member of the crew, not just a bewildered passenger holding on for dear life.

Tentatively his moist right hand released its grip on the bucket seat and probed in his jacket pocket for the *hoja de ruta*. Gingerly he passed the route sheet to his left hand. Now the right hand reached to the glove compartment for a small flashlight. Watch out! Señor Fraga was slackening his speed and shifting down. That meant a power slide around a curve, a struggle between the force of inertia and the sudden shift of direction. Route sheet secure, Pedro gripped the bar under the bucket seat again with his left hand and leaned with the slide.

Señor Fraga came out of the turn onto a straightaway and Pedro completed his move toward the flashlight. Each hand now held an object—the left hand the route sheet, the right hand the flashlight. Watch out! Señor Fraga was shifting down for another turn. Once more Pedro grabbed, holding now to the flashlight as well as to the bucket seat and the route sheet. On the next straightaway Pedro, steadied by his safety belt, was able to shine the thin beam of light on the route sheet. Where were they?

There was Buenos Aires behind them to the southeast. Here was the road to Pergamino and beyond it the road to Venado Tuerto, which meant one-eyed deer. Between Pergamino and Venado Tuerto were the two points Pedro had marked with his pencil, the sharp curve and the railroad crossing. Beyond Venado Tuerto was the third place, the bridge at Rio Cuarto. If all went well they should reach Rio Cuarto at—

Watch out! Señor Fraga was slowing down; his right foot was off the accelerator and pumping the brake pedal. Pedro grabbed everything, flashlight, route sheet, and bucket seat. Which way the skid? He prepared to lean with the drift. Left!

Señor Fraga drifted around a long corner and down a slope. At the foot of the slope on the right was a cluster of lights—a village. They drifted down the slope, tires whining, and cornered nicely into a side street of the village. In front of the cottages stood groups of people—men in pajamas and women with coats or blankets wrapped around nightgowns—standing there cheering and waving.

Pedro was amazed. If he hadn't been so busy holding onto everything he would have waved back. Imagine it, he told himself. People getting out of bed in the middle of the night to see us and cheer us on.

It was heart-warming. It was also short-lived. Señor Fraga stepped on the gas, zoomed down the side street in second gear, skidded around another turn, and roared up and out of the village into the dark and quiet of the countryside. They were racing down a straight road again and Pedro was able to return gingerly to his map reading.

He was careful about it; he was aware of the slackening speed and the diminishing whine of the chords played by the gears each time they shifted down to second. Then Pedro put aside his work and held on, so that the speed and direction of the car could triumph over the force of inertia. At first he had felt like a seasick voyager seated at a pitching table beside a ravenous shipmate. He had made progress. Now he was a sailor high above the deck, dizzily working in the rigging of a sailing ship, with wary eyes on the great waves that were pitching and rolling the vessel.

One was coming. Stop work and hold on! Back to work, but with a wary eye. Lights ho! From the summit of a slope he saw a glow of light on the horizon to the west. Señor Fraga spoke for the first time since Buenos Aires. He said only one word. "Pergamino."

"*Bueno*," said Pedro, and almost added *gracias*.

Consulting the map while the night air rushed by and the engine roared, Pedro could see that the Grand Prix committee had routed the race through the outskirts of the city. There were no wide *avenidas* like *Alvear* or *Uriburu*, just narrow side streets. Señor Fraga slowed down and carefully negotiated them. Faces in the cheering crowd became clearly visible, calls and cheers were audible.

There was not much to be seen of the city of Pergamino, but Pedro found one thing there—his composure. By the time Pergamino was passed he was his old efficient self, once more aware of things like instruments on the dashboard—oil pressure, 55 pounds, water temperature, 150 Fahrenheit. They were okay, but he was shocked to think that he hadn't thought of them sooner. He realized now how affected he had been by the fantastic tension and excitement, as well as Señor Fraga's relentless pressure on the gas pedal.

That pressure was still on as Señor Fraga shifted down, skidded through a turn, shifted up to high, and roared off into the darkened countryside. Checking his route sheet as they surmounted a slope, Pedro saw, with a shiver of excitement, that the first of the points he had penciled—that sharp curve to the right—was a little more than two kilometers ahead.

Pedro spoke up over the roar of the engine and the rush of the night air. "Sharp curve to the right coming up, Señor Fraga—two kilometers."

"Bueno," said Señor Fraga, with a grateful nod of his head.

Pedro felt better; for the first time he felt useful. It was possible that Señor Fraga would have recalled the sharp curve without being reminded of it, but he appreciated it in any case. It showed that his co-pilot was on the job. And it was about time, Pedro told himself. He knew he was a novice in the Grand Prix, but he was determined not to act like one any longer.

One kilometer flew by, then another. Had Señor Fraga forgotten? No. Here was the pressure on the brakes, the slackening of speed, the diminution of sounds from the slowing engine. Slickly and smoothly Señor Fraga was shifting down from high to second, down even further now, all the way down to first. And with good reason. The curve was sharp indeed, its course obscured by trees and clumps of bushes on the right side of the road. Through this foliage flickered the beam of a light, warning them like the beam of a lighthouse—beware of the shoal, beware of the sharp curve.

Señor Fraga was well aware of it. His cornering was almost gentle with respect. The greatly reduced speed gave Pedro a clear picture of the surprising scene that lurked behind the clump of bushes and trees. There in the field beyond the road, on the far side of a shattered fence, was a cluster of people and a damaged racing car, all illuminated by a tow truck's searchlight. Casualty number four!

Pedro's eyes were becoming used to a quick assessment of accidents. He had very little time to look, but in that time he established the fact that the number of the car was 19 and that its two-man crew had walked away from the wreck.

Pedro held the news back until Señor Fraga was in a straight stretch of road. Only then did he report what he had seen. Señor Fraga acknowledged the information with a nod and a brief comment, *"Mala suerte."* Bad luck. That was all. Señor Fraga had known that the curve was a trap, but when a driver was caught in it—too bad.

Meanwhile Car 25, racing through the darkened countryside, had already outdistanced four rivals—Car 23 with Juan Hunter, Car 22 cracked up against the monument, Car 20 in the fountain, and Car 19 spun out on the sharp curve. In a comparatively short space of time and distance Señor Fraga had moved up four places—considerable progress.

Since peeling rubber in front of the Automobile Club in Buenos Aires, Señor Fraga had been exceedingly closemouthed. It was, thought Pedro, an amazing change. Before the race Señor Fraga couldn't keep his mouth shut; now he hardly opened it. At the Automobile Club Pedro had been irritated by Señor Fraga. Now he felt proud of him. He was still feeling that way when an illuminated glance at the route sheet showed that the railroad crossing was coming up. It was, Pedro quickly calculated, three kilometers away.

"Railroad crossing, three kilometers." Pedro spoke the words above the roar of the engine and the rush of the wind.

Rosendo nodded his acknowledgment, but did not slacken his speed. Pedro remembered with a sense of foreboding the *señor's* strategy. Most drivers slowed for railroad crossings. Some even stopped. Señor Fraga had a different idea.

Apprehensively Pedro consulted the route sheet. At the railroad crossing the road curved out gradually onto the tracks, crossed them, and continued straight for a stretch. That would suit Señor Fraga's strategy if it worked.

Pedro flicked the beam of the flashlight at the dashboard. The oil pressure was still up, the water temperature normal. The tachometer was registering the right number of r.p.m.'s. Wait a minute. Check something else. Pedro realized with horror that in his state of tension he had overlooked another dial on the dashboard

—the fuel gauge. He checked it now quickly. The tank was half full. Back to the route sheet flashed the light. Where was the rendezvous for fuel? Here, just this side of the town of Escondido. Quickly calculating the consumption of gas at high speed, Pedro figured that they should have enough to make the rendezvous if all went well.

But so many things had to go well! Señor Fraga had said he was planning to fly over the railroad tracks, a daring procedure against which Pedro's conservative mechanical sense rebelled. Was Señor Fraga under the impression that the car was an airplane? It had no rudder, no ailerons. It was steered by the front wheels gripping the ground. How did Señor Fraga expect to control it when all four wheels were in the air?

Señor Fraga was about to answer the question. Two of the three kilometers had been consumed by the ravenous speed of the car. They were racing into the gradual curve. Unfortunately, there was something already in the curve, an obstacle with two red tail-lights, a dark bulk with a white stripe—a racing car!

Route sheet in one hand, flashlight in the other, Pedro gripped the bucket seat and glanced at Señor Fraga; he saw the smallest of smiles soften the grim line of the mouth under the mustache.

The car ahead was shifting down, slackening speed for the railroad crossing. Car 25 raced through the curve in a beautifully controlled Grand Prix drift. The sound made by the tires seemed now not one of complaint but of triumph. Pedro gripped the seat and stared ahead into the darkness beyond the beam of the headlights. Beyond the beam lay the tracks, silent and invisible.

Nearer now was the other car; the roar of its engine was audible. Car 25 pulled up on its left in passing position. For just a second they raced along together toward the railroad tracks. In that brief time Pedro glanced to the right and the driver of the other car glanced to the left. His look matched Pedro's emotion. It was one of disapproval. This was no place to pass, on a curve in front of railroad tracks! The driver of Car 25 was taking a terrible chance; he must be a madman.

He was an unperturbed madman. Señor Fraga raced by on the left and roared right up to the rise in front of the tracks. *Crunch.* The front wheels of the car struck the rise and took off into the night. *Crunch.* The rear wheels of the car struck the rise and did the same. Señor Fraga, driving at breakneck speed, had made a runway out of the rise. They took off; they were in the air, flying!

Pedro had stopped breathing. He was breathless and he felt weightless; the ground had gone out from under him. He felt sorry for the car. Listen to those poor rear wheels spinning helplessly in the air, all their traction taken away from them! It was not right.

Quickly Pedro glanced to the left. What kind of an airplane pilot did Señor Fraga make? A happy one.

The small smile had turned into a grin. The man was mad!

Crunch. Car 25 landed on the road beyond the tracks. The chassis groaned, the tires sobbed. The car lurched, but the rear wheels grabbed for ground, found it, used it, restored steerageway to the driver, and sent the car spinning forward into the straight stretch of highway.

"*Magnífico!*" cried Señor Fraga ecstatically. Flying obviously had an intoxicating effect on Rosendo. The intoxication was heightened by the fact that another car had been passed.

Pedro recovered some of his composure and enough of his voice to make himself heard. "That car we passed was Number 24."

"*Bueno,*" said Señor Fraga. "That makes five in all, doesn't it?"

"*Sí, señor,*" said Pedro.

"Good," said Rosendo. Then he frowned. "Unfortunately, our friend in Number 21 seems to have done as well."

"Who's that?" said Pedro.

"Rubin Garcia."

"Ah yes," said Pedro. He remembered now. Juan Hunter was in 23—the car that had stalled on the ramp—behind them. Rubin Garcia was in 21. And the other two rivals? Pedro searched his memory. Renaldo Gracciani was in 17. Tomas Schmidt was in 12. Where were they? Up ahead somewhere, racing through the night.

Señor Fraga, grim and silent again, seemed determined to catch them. His right foot kept heavy pressure on the gas pedal while his agile hands skillfully meshed the movement of gears and wheels. Villages flashed by, with clusters of cheering people in blankets and pajamas. Long fields passed more slowly; in them stood farm animals, horses and cows, asleep or gazing with wide and startled eyes into the sudden glare of the headlights.

There were lights ahead now, the wide, bright glow of a city. "Venado Tuerto," announced Señor Fraga. The town of the one-eyed deer.

They were slowing down outside of Venado Tuerto for a control point. They saw a big van with a canopy and a stout official with a brassard on his arm. "Rosendo Fraga," he called out. "Car 25."

"Greetings," cried Rosendo. "Tell me, friend, where is Car 21?"

"Just went through," said the official, and jerked his thick thumb toward the town.

"Good," said Señor Fraga. "We're gaining."

Eeee. Rosendo peeled rubber, waved an arm, and said, "*Hasta luego!*"

Pedro, studying the route sheet, saw that to the west of Venado Tuerto the road became a straightaway for about the next thirty kilometers. He would measure it on the speedometer and warn Señor Fraga when it was due to end, so that they would not spin out on the first curve. He made sure that his seat belt was secure, and steeled himself mentally for the speed he was sure would come.

He thought he was ready for it, but it came with such a rush that it almost overwhelmed him. Only once before, on the Autodrome, had Señor Fraga pushed the car to its fullest polenta. And on the Autodrome such fantastic speed was less sensational, for the race track was designed for it. But this was a plain highway out in the country. Those were just fields on the sides, not stands for spectators. The Autodrome was illuminated; this road was dark except for the glare of the headlights, whose range was sharply reduced by the extreme speed. What might lurk in the darkness ahead as they hurtled toward it? Anything. An obstacle as small as a wayward chicken, as big as a farmer's wagon.

Pedro, straining forward to see, could only hope and pray that the race committee had done its work well and cleared the track. If they hit anything at this speed it would be disastrous. His hands were moist and his heart was pounding again. The engine was raging, the night air screaming. Pedro was fearful of the terrific speed, yet proud of the power the engine was producing. Apprehensively he glanced at the gauges on the dashboard—oil pressure, okay; water temperature, too. The tachometer registered 6500 r.p.m.'s and the needle on the speedometer trembled at 230 k.p.h. *Fantástico.*

Gripping the steel bar under the bucket seat Pedro peered into the night, trying to pierce the blackness beyond the white range of headlights. Two tiny red lights came into his vision—taillights. "Car ahead!" he cried, and gripped the bar with all his might. They were going to crash!

But Señor Fraga had seen the taillights too. He reacted with all the skill that experience and natural ability had given him. He did not jerk the wheel violently to the left. Any movement so abrupt at such a speed would send them screaming into a spin and turn them over.

Señor Fraga had the nerve and the presence of mind to inch the wheel to the left so that the swerve was slight. The skid was almost imperceptible, the maneuver so nicely timed that when the taillights of the car up ahead became bright and red and close, Car 25 was on the left in the open lane.

They did not zoom by this rival. His speed was too great. But they passed steadily, triumphantly, with the number clear on the rival's car, the taut profiles of its driver and pitman visible—Car 21, driven by Rubin Garcia.

"*Hola,* Rubin!" Señor Fraga's cry was triumphant, but not for a second did he take his eyes off the road ahead. They passed and pulled away with the night air screaming around them.

Pedro glanced at the illuminated dials on the dashboard. Oil pressure okay, water temperature okay, r.p.m.'s satisfactory. With the speedometer he calculated that there were just three kilometers left of this straight stretch of road. "Three kilometers left!" he cried above the din.

"*Bueno.*" Señor Fraga nodded. But he did not reduce the terrific speed.

"Two kilometers!" cried Pedro. He wanted to add a warning, but restrained himself.

"*Bueno.*" There seemed to be a small, fiendish smile under Señor Fraga's mustache. What was the madman thinking? Was he planning to plunge Car 25 and its crew to its destruction? Or was he deliberately teasing his pitman?

"One kilometer," announced Pedro lifelessly. Disaster, perhaps death, lay ahead. He gripped the steel bar hard and tried to resign himself to his fate.

Almost immediately the whole car seemed to slump with a sudden slackening of speed. It had been under terrific strain. Now it relaxed like a sprinter who has breasted the tape. As the speed dropped sharply the ferocity went out of the sounds. Pedro could feel the pull of all the brakes and felt proud of their power and efficiency.

Señor Fraga was an airplane pilot again, bringing a jet in for a fast landing on a short strip. He had everything but flaps. He even reversed his engines, in a way, by shifting down to second and using the increased drag of the gears. The gears whined and the tires complained, but the car obediently curved to the right instead of hurtling forward into a field.

As they roared up and out of the turn Pedro relaxed a little. His route sheet showed no more such straightaways before the immediate destination of Rio Cuarto. The race would return to its familiar pattern—spurts of speed in short stretches, Grand Prix drifts in the long, gradual curves, power slides in the sharper turns, and reduced speed for the villages.

They were passing through a village now and Señor Fraga, casually steering with his left hand, reached out with the right, palm upraised, and said, "Salami sandwich, please."

Salami sandwich? Pedro was startled for a second. It seemed so incongruous. But Señor Fraga probably saw it as his reward for catching up with and passing Rubin Garcia in Car 21.

Pedro supplied the sandwich. Señor Fraga's jaws clamped down on it, tore it into edible parts, and chewed *con mucho gusto.*

"Take one for yourself, Pedro." The sentence was muffled with bits of bread and salami.

"Gracias, señor," said Pedro. "A little later." He still had butterflies in his stomach, which would have been unfriendly to the salami.

"Café, por favor." Coffee, please.

Pedro reached for the Thermos and poured a cup of coffee, spilling a little as the car skidded in a corner. Señor Fraga, holding the rest of his sandwich in his teeth, had started a power slide. He roared up and out of the turn, shifted to high, finished his sandwich, and reached for his coffee. As he drank it he sped down a short stretch, and said, "Another sandwich, please."

"*Sí, señor*," said Pedro, marveling at the driver's appetite and the dexterity of his maneuvers with wheel and gearshift, clutch and brake, salami and coffee.

Pedro drank a cup of *café* and felt better. He decided to try a sandwich. That, too, had a buoyant effect. He began to feel like his old self again. His mind was able to overcome his apprehension and think with more detachment. When Señor Fraga had spoken of the strain and stress of the Grand Prix, it had been hard for Pedro to visualize it. Now as a novice he had gone through it—some of it, at least. From now on certain experiences would be repetitive and his reactions would be better because of it. He was sure of that. He was also sure that there would be new experiences, thrilling, shocking, and surprising. Somehow he would have to find the strength to survive them. He was already stronger, he felt. You either got stronger and stayed in the race or you got weaker and gave up.

They raced on through the night, maintaining their lead over the cars they had passed. They skidded, drifted, and spurted. The engine roared; the gears sang up and down the scale; the tires harmonized. And almost imperceptively a gray light from the east, which gradually illuminated the fields and farmhouses and villages, stole over their shoulders. Objects that had

125

been dark and mysterious became identifiable—a wagon here, cattle there. Blue smoke was rising out of cottage chimneys and a white mist from the fields. A cock crowed, the gray light brightened, and behind them rose the sun over the pampas, the plains of Argentina.

CHAPTER 7

As THEY raced along the road with the sun rising behind them, Pedro consulted his route sheet and saw another place he had marked with his pencil. A fuel stop was coming up soon. It had to be, for the needle on the fuel gauge was dipping down dangerously near *E* for *empty*.

The route sheet showed a road curving into Escondido, a village five kilometers to the east. The gasoline truck was to be stationed on the curve before the town. "Fuel stop coming up," Pedro announced, "five kilometers."

Señor Fraga acknowledged the announcement with a nod and glanced at the fuel gauge. Was he alarmed by the position of the needle? If so, he didn't show it. But he would certainly be worried if the fuel truck were not at the rendezvous.

The sun climbed a little higher and shone far ahead

on an object toward which they were speeding. Small at first, the object grew in size. By the time Señor Fraga took his foot off the accelerator, the object was enormous, but as friendly-looking as an oasis in a desert —the fuel truck, waiting for them.

Young men in coveralls gathered around Car 25. Their attitude was admiring and attentive. Eager hands unscrewed the top to the fuel tank and pumped in gas.

"Almost empty, eh?" said the leader of the crew.

"Of course," said Señor Fraga. "At the speed I drive, this rocket gulps gas." He placed a cigarette in his silver holder.

"Sorry, sir," said the leader of the fuel crew apologetically. "No smoking."

"Don't worry, *amigo*," said Señor Fraga heartily. "I won't light up until you finish."

Pedro was hustling about checking tire pressure, touching the brake drums to see if they were too hot, peering under the hood. He was busy, yet he couldn't help but hear the conversation between Señor Fraga and the crew.

Gesturing with both hands, Señor Fraga was describing their crossing of the railroad tracks. "I made a ski jump out of the tracks," he boasted. "We flew through the air, didn't we, Pedro?"

"*Sí, señor,*" said Pedro, kneeling and checking the pressure in the right front tire.

With graceful gestures Señor Fraga described how

he took the sharp curve while a competitor spun out. The fuel crew listened appreciatively. Señor Fraga was in fine form in front of this audience.

The attendant at the fuel tank was removing the hose. "That should do it," he said. "Check your gauge."

Pedro hustled to the dashboard and switched on the ignition. The needle on the gauge climbed from E and trembled to a stop at F. "Full," said Pedro. "Seventy gallons."

"*Bueno*," said Señor Fraga. He thought of something he had almost forgotten. "By the way, *amigos,* have you seen Gracciani in Car 17?"

"*Sí*," said the leader of the crew. "He stopped here just before you."

"Good," said Señor Fraga. "We'll catch him before Rio Cuarto. *Venga,* Pedro, *vamos!*"

Pedro was already in his bucket seat, safety belt buckled.

"*Adios, amigos!*" Señor Fraga gave a gallant wave, stabbed at the accelerator, revved up the engine, and snapped out the clutch.

Eeee. Señor Fraga peeled rubber and Car 25 roared off into the night. Once again Señor Fraga changed and became the quiet, skillful driver at the wheel. The performance at the fuel stop was obviously over.

Not too long after the fuel stop they raced up over a slope and skidded through a turn at the top. Behind them stretched the pampas, before them a wide river sparkling in the rising sun. Rio Cuarto.

Pedro glanced at his wrist watch. "It's almost ten minutes to eight," he said.

"Good time," said Señor Fraga, but he spoke in a listless voice. Fine lines of fatigue pulled at the corners of his eyes and mouth. He looked worn out. And with good reason, thought Perdo—almost eight solid hours of driving at breakneck speed. In Rio Cuarto there would be a two-hour rest. Señor Fraga looked as if he needed it. In fact, he looked as if he wanted to take it right here on the east side of the Rio Cuarto.

Then something happened, a combination of things. A cheer from a crowd on a corner refreshed the driver. A glimpse of another car up ahead provoked him. The memory of a familiar obstacle, the bridge over the river, stimulated him. He stepped on the gas.

The car up ahead was slowing down for the bridge over the Rio Cuarto. Señor Fraga took advantage of its slower speed and zoomed by. The crowd roared its approval. Pedro stiffened with alarm. We're going to miss the bridge—we're going to plunge into the river!

Suddenly, skillfully, Señor Fraga shifted down, put the car into a drift, and skidded out onto the bridge.

We made it! thought Pedro, with a surge of relief.

Señor Fraga gunned the engine and raced triumphantly across the river to the city of Rio Cuarto. Behind them, chagrined, came the driver of the car they had just passed—Renaldo Gracciani in Car 17.

Crowds were cheering, Señor Fraga was smiling, officials with arm bands were waiting in the plaza. To

Pedro it felt like the finish line. There was a sudden surge of relief from tension. His fingers trembled a little and his legs seemed unsteady as he got out of the car. I've survived, he told himself. It didn't seem possible that they had come through in one piece. Nor did something else seem possible—that the race was just beginning. This fantastic lap from Buenos Aires to Rio Cuarto was just the beginning, not the end. In only two hours they would be roaring away again toward the snow-capped Andes to the west and the mountain city of Mendoza.

For one weak moment Pedro wished that the race were over, that Rio Cuarto were the end of the line. Then that wish was swept away in all the noise and organized confusion. Señor Fraga was shaking a welcoming hand here, kissing an admiring cheek there, and accepting compliments with unconcealed delight. And being interviewed: Yes, he had moved up several places in the standings. How many cars had he passed? Let's see now. Six—no, seven. Competitively, did Señor Fraga think he had done as well as any other driver in the first twenty? Would he mind stepping over here for a picture? Leaning up against the car like that was fine.

"Pedro." Señor Fraga's sonorous voice cut through the chaos.

"*Sí, señor.*"

"Over here. Picture for the press."

Pedro protested. "But I did nothing, *señor.*"

"Nonsense," said Señor Fraga generously. "You gave

the car the polenta I used in that straight stretch where we passed Rubin Garcia." He was talking to a reporter again, then to a photographer, then to an official. Almost in the same breath he was suggesting breakfast.

Breakfast? thought Pedro. What about those salami sandwiches?

As if he had heard Pedro's thought Señor Fraga said, "I have the appetite of a bear in these races. I burn up energy like a car burns gas."

An extraordinary man, Señor Fraga. And generous. He had pulled his pitman into the picture and mentioned the polenta. Señor Fraga was not taking all the credit.

"*Vamos!*" Señor Fraga had his arm around Pedro's shoulder. By this time there were several others, all invited to breakfast by Señor Fraga.

"But *señor,*" Pedro protested, "I'd like to work on the car."

"No-no-no." Rosendo ran his negatives together as if they were all one word. "You can't work on the car, Pedro. This plaza is a *parque cerrado*. It won't be open at all for work on the engines. Come along, my boy—breakfast."

Reluctantly Pedro went along. It disturbed him to leave the car in the *parque cerrado,* although it was well watched by officials. In fact one of them was even lifting the hood, looking at the engine.

Pedro started to protest, but Señor Fraga intervened. "Calm down, Pedro. He is an inspector making sure we have nothing illegal on the car. Let him look—that's his privilege. You and I will relax. One becomes tenser than one thinks, eh? Come along."

Pedro went along. He felt outmaneuvered. The car was in the *parque cerrado,* its engine being inspected, and he was being told tactfully that he was tense and should relax. Well, perhaps Señor Fraga was right.

They ate breakfast in the dining room of the Hotel de Roma, where Señor Fraga had reserved a room with twin beds. "After breakfast," said Rosendo, wiping egg off his mouth, "we will go up to the room and rest. We both need it."

"*Sí, señor,*" said Pedro, eating his steak and eggs. Señor Fraga was probably right. He had been right recently about many things, about the sharp curve, the straightaway, and the bridge over the Rio Cuarto. He was talking now about these triumphs to his friends, who were car dealers in Rio Cuarto. They were listening intently, making the right noises at the right times, sucking in their breaths with surprise, letting out laughs. Señor Fraga was in the center of the stage again and enjoying his own performance. Between lines he was smacking his lips over egg-smeared steak, munching toast, and swallowing coffee.

Pedro had heard it all before, but he didn't mind the repetition. He had not realized how hungry he was, and he was happily enjoying his breakfast. Señor Fraga had been right to insist on eating. Now, glancing at his watch, Señor Fraga announced that it was time for his siesta. "Come along, Pedro, let's go up to our room and rest."

Señor Fraga was yawning. He looked tired. But breakfast had stimulated Pedro. He didn't feel like resting. He wanted to get back to the car to be sure nothing happened to it.

Señor Fraga laughed somewhat impatiently. "I told you, Pedro, this *parque cerrado* is not open at all for engine work."

Pedro had an inspiration. "Couldn't I switch the tires?" he said.

"Yes," Señor Fraga conceded, "you could do that." He yawned and again glanced at his watch. "What time do you have, Pedro?"

"Eight-forty-eight."

"Right," said Rosendo. "Our starting time will be earlier from Rio Cuarto, because we have moved up seven places. Seven places in one lap, Pedro!"

"*Sí, señor,*" said Pedro, with enthusiasm.

"Which means," said Señor Fraga, "that we shall leave Rio Cuarto at eighteen minutes past ten. Therefore I will sleep for about an hour, and meet you at the *parque cerrado* at nine-fifty-five."

Pedro felt a twitch of warning. "Will that give us enough time, *señor?*"

"Certainly," said Rosendo. "We won't be late. Don't worry, my boy." He patted Pedro on the back. "Go ahead, Pedro. Switch the tires. Then stroll around the city. Take in the sights. Flirt with the pretty girls."

Señor Fraga chuckled. "Don't forget, my boy, you're a hero—a copilot and pitman in the Grand Prix. There are plenty of pretty girls in Rio Cuarto who would be delighted to have a cup of coffee with you in a *confitería.*"

Pretty girls. The mere mention of them seemed to kindle a fire in Señor Fraga's face. But it was a flash fire, dying as quickly as it flared up, leaving his face looking worn out. He yawned cavernously. "And so to bed," he said. "*Hasta luego.*"

"Until later," said Pedro.

Later. Where? In the *parque cerrado* at nine-fifty-five. But they were leaving at ten-eighteen. That wasn't allowing much time, and Señor Fraga looked as if he should have at least two hours of sleep instead of just one. He should have had less breakfast and less congenial conversation with his *compañeros.*

But Señor Fraga was wise in many ways. His strategy in the race had been flawless. His reservation of a room at the Hotel de Roma showed foresight. I must mind my own business, thought Pedro.

Returning to the *parque cerrado,* Pedro switched the tires, right front to left rear, left front to right rear. He checked the air pressure of all the tires, including the spares. Then he looked at his watch. Nine-thirty. He had time for a stroll outside the *parque cerrado.*

"Are you Pedro Thompson?"

Pedro swung around, startled, and saw two men in

135

coveralls. The man who spoke was familiar. Where had Pedro seen that fair face before?

A hand was extended. "I'm Juan Hunter." He smiled. "You remember, Car 23. We stalled at the start in Buenos Aires."

"Oh yes," said Pedro, a little embarrassed for Señor Hunter's sake. "That was bad luck."

Señor Hunter shrugged his shoulders. "It could happen to anyone. Let me introduce my younger brother, Pablo."

As Pedro shook hands with Pablo, Señor Hunter said, "I thought you two should meet. Rosendo tells me you are something of an athlete, Pedro. So is my kid brother. Perhaps you can get a workout together."

"Fine," said Pedro. He became more eager. "As a matter of fact, I brought along my soccer ball. Do you play, Pablo?"

"Certainly," said the younger brother.

"Good," said Pedro. "When we get time, in Mendoza, perhaps?"

"Fine," said Pablo. "*Con mucho gusto.*"

Juan Hunter changed the subject. "Where is that pilot of yours?"

"At the Hotel de Roma," said Pedro.

"Ah!" cried Señor Hunter. "And asleep, too, I'll bet."

Pedro said nothing. As far as he was concerned Señor Fraga's fatigue and his siesta were a team secret.

"Don't forget to wake him up," said Señor Hunter.

He turned to his younger brother. "Come on, Pablo, we've got to go."

"*Hasta la vista,* Pedro."

"*Hasta luego.*"

Pedro was delighted to meet Pablo Hunter, but he was a little disturbed by Juan Hunter's remark about Señor Fraga. Would it be necessary to wake him up? Pedro hoped it wouldn't be. He glanced at his wrist watch. Nine-forty. Señor Fraga had promised to arrive at the *parque cerrado* at nine-fifty-five. He still had fifteen minutes, and the Hotel de Roma was only a five-minute walk away. But Señor Fraga had been very tired. Suppose he overslept and didn't wake up until ten, or ten past ten? The ground so daringly gained the night before would be wiped out. *Caray!*

Señor Hunter was aware of this, doubly aware of it because he had lost several places by stalling on the ramp at Buenos Aires. He knew that Señor Fraga could do the same by simply oversleeping at the Hotel de Roma in Rio Cuarto. *Diablos!*

Pedro had nothing to do. Mechanical work, which usually took his mind off his worries, was forbidden. And the appearance of other pilots and copilots increased his worry. These teams were ready to go. Where was Señor Fraga? Still asleep at the Hotel de Roma! And the minutes were ticking by—nine-forty-five, nine-fifty. All around Pedro now in the *parque cerrado* drivers were stepping on starters, revving up engines. Each snarl and growl increased Pedro's apprehension.

He stood it as long as he could; then he set out for the Hotel de Roma. He did not walk—he ran. It was not quite yet nine-fifty-five, but Pedro had a nerve-racking suspicion that Señor Fraga was still in the sack.

Rosendo's room was on the second floor of the hotel. Pedro ignored the elevator and went up the stairs two at a time. His fist sounded like a burned-out bearing as he knocked on the door.

Silence. He knocked again, louder.

A muffled voice answered, "Who is it?"

"It's me, Pedro."

"What do you want?" The voice was irritable.

What do I want! Pedro felt like shouting. Instead he said, "It's late, Señor Fraga! It's time to go. You overslept."

Pedro heard a groan, a growl, and a few muttered curses. Then the door opened and Señor Fraga stood there in his silk pajamas, puffy-eyed and slack-jawed, with a stubble of beard on his annoyed face. "What time is it?" he growled.

"Ten o'clock!" cried Pedro.

"*Diablos!*" cred Señor Fraga. "I have to shower and shave." He started for the bathroom.

"You don't have time," said Pedro, with a curtness that surprised himself.

Señor Fraga stopped. He swung around and glared at his pitman.

Pedro held up his wrist watch and stood his ground. Señor Fraga continued to the bathroom, but when he reached it he simply splashed water on his face. Towel in hand, he cried, "All right, I'll skip the shave and shower, but get me a cup of coffee—*pronto*."

"*Sí, señor,*" said Pedro. He ran to the phone and called for the coffee. Then he thought of something else. Coffee for the Thermos jugs—and they were in the car. *Diablos!* And if Señor Fraga didn't have time for breakfast some bread or rolls had better be taken along too. First Pedro packed Señor Fraga's suitcase and snapped it shut.

The waiter arrived with the coffee, and Pedro gave his order for additional coffee and a bag of rolls.

"*Sí, señor,*" said the waiter. Pedro was briefly pleased. It was the first time in his life that someone had said "*Sí, señor,*" to him; usually Pedro said it to someone else. Such was Grand Prix prestige.

Señor Fraga gulped his coffee and burned his esophagus. "*Diablos!*" he growled.

"*Vamos!*" cried Pedro.

"Coming!" said Señor Fraga. He glanced in a mirror. "I look like the devil," he said.

What does it matter how you look? thought Pedro.

As they hurried downstairs he glanced at his watch. "Eight past ten," he said. "We'd better run."

Señor Fraga rebelled. "And get there exhausted?" he said. "Nonsense, Pedro, we can make it in five minutes."

139

"We must walk fast then," said Pedro, and set out briskly, carrying the coffee in a canister and the rolls in a bag.

"All right," said Señor Fraga. "But we will walk all the same."

It was the longest five-minute walk Pedro had ever taken.

By the time they reached the *parque cerrado* Señor Fraga seemed somewhat like his old self again. The coffee and the brisk walk had pulled him out of the sour mood that had followed his siesta. The roar of the engines and the cheers of the crowd helped revive him. Señor Fraga touched up the silk scarf knotted at his neck. He smiled at a pretty girl, waved to a friend. The rest he had enjoyed was coming to his rescue. His congenial mood returned. "Pedro, my boy," he said, "forgive me for being, er, not quite myself on awakening."

"Certainly, *señor*," said Pedro.

Señor Fraga was now pushing the starter button in the most casual manner, while Pedro held his breath hoping that the engine would respond. The spark exploded, and Pedro breathed a sigh of relief. Casually Señor Fraga revved up the engine. With the same nonchalance he maneuvered the car up to the starting line. All around them raged turbulence—the roaring of engines and the cheering of the crowd. In the eye of the hurricane Señor Fraga sat at his ease, left elbow resting on the car door, right hand toying with the wheel, and now a smile and a wisecrack for the starter.

The starter's flag went up. "Ten seconds."

Señor Fraga's personality seemed to change again. Cast off was the mask of nonchalance; on went the mask of concentration—his eyes narrowed, his jaw line tightened, and his right foot stabbed at the accelerator.

"Tres-dos-uno!" The flag dropped.

Eeee. Señor Fraga snapped out the clutch, stepped on the gas, and peeled rubber. Pedro recovered from the lunge and glanced to his left. Señor Fraga was the picture of concentration. Forgotten were the crowd and the cheers. All that seemed to matter now were the curves and the straight stretches and the maximum speed at which they could be taken.

Pedro tried to settle back in his bucket seat and match Señor Fraga's mood, to concentrate completely on the race—the route to San Luis, then the winding roads up through the foothills of the Andes to the mountain city of Mendoza. But in between minutes of concentration Pedro thought of other things.

What kind of a man was Señor Fraga? The question worried Pedro. The mysterious man on the left seemed completely absorbed in his work, and skillful and daring in its execution. On the road to San Luis he spurted by Car 16. On a straight stretch west of San Luis he caught Car 15 on a curve and passed it. There was no doubt about it; Rosendo Fraga had the ability to command breathless admiration. But Pedro had seen other traits that were disturbing. He wondered

141

how many more the Grand Prix would bring out—and what they would be like—and how he would cope with them.

Meanwhile he traced the course of the car on the route sheet. He kept track of all the gauges on the dashboard—the speedometer and the tachometer, the gauges for fuel, oil, and water pressure. As the car climbed up to Mendoza, Pedro changed the oil, using the hand pump on the dashboard. As the engine heated up dangerously, he pumped fresh water into the radiator.

He was efficient as a pitman. Gone was the apprehension he had experienced on the lap from Buenos Aires to Rio Cuarto. He no longer doubted his competence. What worried him now was the mysterious human element so dramatically represented by the unpredictable personality of Rosendo Fraga.

"Magnifico!" Rosendo Fraga was complimenting the city of Mendoza.

Pedro agreed. Mendoza had a beautiful appearance. It sparkled in the spring sun; it was clean, cool, and clear. To the west towered the snow-capped Andes. In the vicinity of the city nestled vineyards and fields of sugar cane.

On arriving in Mendoza many of the drivers and their pitmen carried their suitcases into the drab army barracks near the *parque cerrado*. Here again Señor Fraga showed his foresight. He had reserved a large room with a pleasant balcony at the Hotel Provincial, a structure of Spanish colonial design with a red tile roof.

"Nothing but the best for us, Pedro," cried Rosendo, clapping his pitman on the shoulder.

Pedro's worries had disappeared. Mendoza looked like a wonderful city. Its inhabitants were enthusiastic about the Grand Prix. The Hotel Provincial was excellent. Car 25 was running well. And Señor Fraga was in the best of spirits.

The phone rang in their room. Señor Fraga answered it. "For you, Pedro."

"For me?" said Pedro. "I don't know anyone in Mendoza."

It was Pablo Hunter, asking Pedro about exercise. Apparently other pitmen wanted a workout, too. If Pedro could bring along his soccer ball, there was a fine field right behind the barracks.

Pedro was delighted. "Would you like to come, Señor Fraga?"

Señor Fraga chuckled. "No, thank you, Pedro. My knee, you know. And I'm tired. I'm going to finish the siesta I started in Rio Cuarto."

"Of course," said Pedro, using one of Señor Fraga's fondest expressions.

Señor Fraga smiled. "You go ahead, Pedro. You young bloods have all the energy. Besides"—he arched his eyebrows—"you must remember that we veterans have been doing all the driving so far."

"I'll be glad to drive any time," said Pedro eagerly.

Señor Fraga yawned. "I'm saving you for the mountains, Pedro."

Rosendo took his silk pajamas from his suitcase and tossed them on a twin bed. Then he strolled out on the balcony, yawned, and stretched. "Mendoza," he said sonorously, "a beautiful city. There's a fine restaurant here, Pedro, just as good as La Mimosa in Buenos Aires, and a *confitería* as lively as any in the capital. We'll celebrate tonight, Pedro, eh, just a little? Tomorrow's Sunday, a day off."

"Not for me," said Pedro. "Tomorrow morning there is no race, so the regulations allow pitmen to work in the *parque cerrado*. Remember?"

"Ah yes," said Señor Fraga. He turned back into the room, picked up his pajamas, and smiled. "Well, that's fair enough. It was my turn today—yours tomorrow." He yawned again. "I'm tired, Pedro, dead tired." He rubbed the stubble on his face. "I should shave," he mumbled, "but I don't have the energy."

Quickly Señor Fraga undressed, put on his pajamas, and got into bed. *"Hasta la vista,"* he said, and closed his eyes.

"Hasta la vista," said Pedro.

Quietly Pedro unpacked his own suitcase. Neatly he put his pajamas on his bed, his leather kit in the bathroom. Then he left the room on tiptoe, closing the door quietly behind him and shutting out the snores of Señor Fraga.

144

Rosendo was exhausted. Well, why shouldn't he be? He had driven all the way from Buenos Aires to Mendoza at super speeds. Quite a performance. He had improved his position by nine places! That meant they would be leaving Mendoza as number fourteen instead of twenty-five. Think of it!

Señor Fraga should be exhausted. Let him sleep as long as he liked. He had earned a long rest; he was a hero.

So thought Pedro as he hurried to the *parque cerrado*. There he unpacked the soccer ball, inflated it, and carried it briskly to the army barracks and the room occupied by Pablo Hunter.

Pablo Hunter had gathered together a group of younger pitmen. They had a fine time kicking the ball back and forth on the army field. Pedro returned to the hotel healthily tired, and found Señor Fraga still asleep. Pedro showered and shaved. Señor Fraga was still asleep, and it was almost time for dinner.

The phone rang and Pedro answered. It was Señor Rodriguez, a car dealer in Mendoza and a friend of Señor Fraga. "He's still asleep? Wake him up."

"But, *señor*," Pedro protested.

"He's having dinner with me in half an hour," said Señor Rodriguez, "and so are you."

"Oh," said Pedro. "Thank you, *señor*."

"*De nada*," said Señor Rodriguez. "Now wake him up. I'll call back."

"Señor Fraga!" called Pedro. No luck. Gently Pedro

shook the sleeper. Rosendo stirred, and mumbled, "Not enough polenta." Pedro shook a little harder. Señor Fraga cursed and opened his eyes. "What do you want?" he growled.

"Señor Rodriguez just called," said Pedro. "He expects us for dinner in half an hour."

"*Diablos!*" cried Señor Fraga. "Is it that late?" He yawned, stretched, and stumbled to the bathroom, his eyes half-closed and his bearded jowls drooping.

He still needs sleep, thought Pedro.

Señor Fraga shaved, showered, and emerged looking better. He dressed and looked better still. His eyes began to sparkle. He smiled. "*Vamos!*" he cried. "The siesta is over. Now for the *fiesta.*"

"*Fiesta?*" said Pedro.

"It's Saturday night," said Señor Fraga happily, "and a day off tomorrow. We must celebrate."

"Celebrate what, *señor?*" said Pedro. After all, the race had just started. Moreover, Pedro was beginning to feel tired. He yawned.

Señor Fraga looked hurt. "Celebrate our performance, Pedro." He spoke with a certain coolness in his tone. "We've done rather well, Pedro, not just for the number of cars passed, but in elapsed time too."

Pedro realized he had been tactless. "*Sí, señor,*" he said quickly. "You've done very well, very well indeed."

Señor Fraga gave a gratified grunt.

It was not idle flattery, thought Pedro. Señor Fraga had done well; he was entitled to a little relaxation.

That was the phrase Pedro took with him as he accompanied Señor Fraga to dinner with Señor Rodriguez and several friends. They were all in the automobile business; they were all congenial and hospitable. Numerous glasses of wine were filled—"the fine wine of Mendoza."

Could Señor Fraga refuse to drink a glass of "the fine wine of Mendoza"? It would be tactless. He was supposed to be in training, but he was a guest of these good citizens of Mendoza.

Señor Fraga was describing his flight over the railroad tracks. Señor Rodriguez lifted his glass of wine. "That calls for a toast—to the flight over the railroad tracks."

More wine was poured. Another highlight of the race was toasted, and still another. Pedro began to worry. This was going too far. But what can I say? he thought. Señor Fraga is certainly old enough to take care of himself. Moreover, he is the captain of our team as well as its financier. I'm just the junior member and a novice at that. Pedro ate his dinner, drank his milk, and kept quiet.

After a long and increasingly noisy dinner the group decided to adjourn to a *confitería*.

"I'm going to bed, Señor Fraga," Pedro announced, and dared to add, "How about you, *señor?*"

Rosendo laughed and clapped Pedro on the back.

"Did you hear that, *compañeros?* Did you hear what my trainer said?"

The gay group laughed, and Pedro felt a twinge of irritation. Señor Fraga made a few more jovial remarks and aimed another whack at Pedro's back. Pedro side-stepped. Señor Fraga missed and lost his balance, but quickly regained it with nimble footwork.

"*Bravo!*" cried Señor Rodriguez. "Nice footwork, Rosendo."

"As fast with his feet as with his words."

"A wonderful sense of timing."

"Marvelous reflexes."

"*Gracias, compañeros!*" cried Rosendo happily. To Pedro he said, "All right, son, run along now and get your sleep. Remember, you didn't take a siesta as I did. Don't worry, my boy, I'll be in by curfew time."

"*Buenas noches, señores,*" said Pedro, and added politely, "*y muchas gracias.*"

"*Buenas noches,* Pedro," chorused the group.

Pedro was glad to leave. The conduct of Señor Fraga was a disappointment. It was most fortunate that there was no race in the morning.

In the Hotel Provincial Pedro was asleep almost as soon as his head touched the pillow.

CHAPTER 8

BROKEN GLASS tinkled. Pedro sat up with a start. He had been dreaming of the race, and he thought at first that Señor Fraga had spun out on a curve. Then he remembered where he was, in the hotel at Mendoza. The room was dark except for a sliver of light stealing out of the bathroom. Señor Fraga must be in there.

"Are you all right, *señor?*" said Pedro.

Señor Fraga's voice came through the door. "The glass slipped. Sorry I woke you up."

"That's all right," said Pedro. He turned on the light by his bed and glanced at his wrist watch. He stared again in disbelief. The hands pointed to three-thirty A.M. What kind of a curfew hour was that!

Pedro was appalled and strongly tempted to express his disapproval. On second thought he decided against it. Undoubtedly Señor Fraga would be in no mood to receive a reproof from the junior member of his team.

The bathroom door opened, the light went out, and Señor Fraga stumbled to bed. In no time at all he was asleep and snoring.

Pedro listened. Snoring, Rosendo sounded as if he had blown a gasket. But Señor Fraga needed an overhaul not so much on his nasal passages as on his brain cells. Pedro's teammate, so daring and skillful at times, was, in a way, a *tonto*, a fool. How much of a fool? So much of one that he would endanger his hard-won standing in the Grand Prix?

That question, and Señor Fraga's snoring, kept Pedro awake for a while. He got up, nevertheless, at seven. Señor Fraga was still asleep, his head half-buried beneath the pillow. Pedro dressed and left quietly. A good breakfast revived his spirits. The *parque cerrado* was open and engine work allowed. It made Pedro feel better. He concentrated on the ignition and the timing. The engine looked and sounded solid and reliable, a true and trusted friend, in sharp contrast to the unpredictable man who drove it.

Pedro finished his work, arranged with Pablo Hunter for another game on the soccer field, and returned to the Hotel Provincial. Señor Fraga was still asleep.

Pedro washed up, changed his clothes, and started out for lunch.

"Pedro?" Rosendo's voice sounded like a voice from a tomb.

Pedro turned. *"Sí, señor."*

"What time is it?"

"Almost one o'clock."

"*Diablos!*" Señor Fraga struggled up to a sitting position and rubbed his bearded jowls. "My head aches. My tongue is thick. All that smoke in the *confitería.*"

"*Sí, señor.*"

Señor Fraga yawned. "Where are you going, Pedro?"

"To lunch."

"*Bueno.* I will meet you downstairs in the dining room."

"*Sí, señor.*"

Pedro had almost finished his lunch by the time Rosendo appeared. He looked far better than he had in bed, but his rather pale complexion was marred by red blotches. "Razor rash," he explained.

Nor was his appetite up to normal. He seemed content with fruit juice and a pot of *café.* His hand shook slightly as he lifted his cup.

What Señor Fraga needs, thought Pedro, is some fresh air and outdoor exercise. Aloud he said, "We have a little soccer game going this afternoon. Would you join us, *señor?*"

Rosendo winced. "Thank you just the same, Pedro." He tapped his right knee. "My knee is acting up."

"I'm sorry," said Pedro. But wasn't it the left knee? Could Señor Fraga be making this up?

Señor Fraga shrugged his shoulders. "It is nothing serious. The effect of the mountain air probably. I have a little sinus trouble, too."

"I am sorry to hear it," said Pedro.

Another shrug. Señor Fraga smiled bravely. "We must take the good with the bad."

"Why don't you come and watch the game, *señor?*" said Pedro. "It is such a beautiful day."

"Some other time," said Señor Fraga. "Today I think I'll just take it easy. Read the papers. Take a siesta."

Another siesta? thought Pedro. Señor Fraga's life off the track seemed to be divided between siestas and *fiestas.* Still Señor Fraga, at his age, must know how best to recuperate from the strain and stress of Mendoza night life.

Pedro walked from the Hotel Provincial to the army barracks, enjoying the city of Mendoza—its clear, cool air, its pleasant plazas, and the snow sparkling on the towering Andes. It was too bad that Señor Fraga could not enjoy this too, but had to spend so much time in siestas.

When Pedro returned from his workout, Señor Fraga was in bed reading the Sunday paper. He smacked it triumphantly. "Did you see, Pedro? We got quite a write-up. I forgot to tell you, my boy, I was interviewed last night in the *confitería.* Listen to this." Señor Fraga read aloud in a sonorous voice, " 'Rosendo Fraga, prominent car dealer from Buenos Aires, driving Car 25, made excellent progress in the first lap of the Grand Prix, going from position twenty-five to position fourteen.' "

"Fine," said Pedro. But where was the "we" in the write-up? The only person mentioned was the driver.

"Pedro."

"*Sí, señor.*"

"In my leather kit in the bathroom is a pair of scissors. Hand them to me, please. I want to clip this story in the paper." He smiled. "A good advertisement, you know."

"Of course," said Pedro. It was convenient, that phrase.

Señor Fraga cut out the clipping, then climbed out of bed and sauntered out onto the balcony. He stretched. "Isn't it a beautiful city? Marvelous! Look at those magnificent mountains. Ah, this is the nicest time of day, my boy, sunset—so much better than sunrise."

"The sunrise, too, is magnificent," said Pedro.

"I suppose so," said Señor Fraga. He returned to the room and reread the clipping. *"Diablos!"* he cried. "That blasted reporter did not mention you, Pedro. I told him what a fine job you had done with the engine."

"It doesn't matter," said Pedro. He wondered if Señor Fraga were telling the truth. Señor Fraga wasn't really a liar, at least not a malicious one. He was more of a fabricator. His trick knee changed from left to right. He blamed his headache on smoke instead of Mendoza wine, just as he blamed the blotches on his face on razor rash.

But the blotches had disappeared and Señor Fraga's fingers, steadied by the siesta, were now deftly trimming his mustache. Rosendo seemed to have recovered from his exertions of the day and night. He was buoyant and congenial again. Pedro hoped Señor Fraga would not become too congenial and stay up half the night with his friends.

Apparently Rosendo anticipated Pedro's apprehension. With a friendly slap on Pedro's shoulder, he said, "Tonight will be a different story, Pedro. Old Rosendo is going to bed early, friends or no friends."

But when the friends appeared and the atmosphere became gay again, Rosendo appeared to forget his good resolutions. When glasses of Mendoza wine were lifted in a toast to the next day's race, Rosendo joined in. Another toast lifted, another glass of wine.

Pedro began to despair. It was getting late and Señor Fraga was getting gayer. Pedro became desperate. He had to act. If he didn't, all was lost. If he did, all might be lost too, but the chance had to be taken.

Quietly Pedro got Señor Fraga's attention. It was not easy, for Rosendo was talking loudly and with great animation. Gently Pedro tugged at the sleeve of Señor Fraga's sports jacket.

Rosendo frowned. "What do you want?"

Pedro swallowed hard and spoke in a low voice. "I think, Señor Fraga—if you don't mind my saying so—it is getting a little late. We ought to be on our way."

Señor Fraga gave Pedro an arrogant look. Carefree,

congenial Rosendo of the *confitería* was caught in the act, and he didn't like it. He started to say something short and rude. Then he apparently thought better of it.

"All right," he said coldly, and he glanced at his watch. "We'll leave in five minutes."

Would he? Pedro wondered and worried. He didn't like the idea of reminding Señor Fraga that his five minutes were up. Pedro sat on the edge of his chair while glasses clinked and the boisterous talk babbled on.

Four minutes went by. Five. Señor Fraga emptied his glass, put out his cigarette, and said, "Gentlemen, how time flies in your congenial company! It is almost ten o'clock and Pedro and I have an appointment early in the morning. Isn't that so, Pedro?" The tone of his voice had a tease to it.

"Sí, señor," said Pedro.

"Don't go yet, Rosendo!" There was a chorus of voices. "The night is still young."

"The night is young," said Rosendo with a smile. "But I am getting older. And as I get older I find it a little harder to get up early in the morning. Isn't that so, Pedro?" Again his tone of voice was teasing.

"I don't know, *señor,*" said Pedro tactfully.

"I do," said Rosendo. He rose. *"Buenas noches, amigos."*

"Adios, Rosendo! *Buena suerte!"*

In their hotel room, Señor Fraga was silent and

aloof. Gone was the gay and congenial *caballero* of the *confitería*. Rosendo was glum. Ahead of him loomed a dismal departure at six A.M. and a day of cold and exacting mountain driving. How different and wonderful seemed the start from Buenos Aires with the great crowds cheering!

The Grand Prix was getting down to business now, grim, cold business, and it was evident that Señor Fraga didn't want to get down to business with it; he preferred the camaraderie of the *confiterías*. He was reluctant to make the social sacrifices that the stress and strain of the Grand Prix required.

To Pedro now came the full realization of what he had got himself into when he signed up with Rosendo Fraga, the gay *caballero* of Buenos Aires.

At precisely five o'clock in the morning Pedro got up, washed his face, brushed his teeth, and woke up Señor Fraga.

It was cold. Señor Fraga shivered and went back to sleep.

Pedro got dressed and woke up Señor Fraga for the second time. Señor Fraga struggled out of bed and stumbled into the bathroom. Pedro went downstairs to the dining room where a special breakfast was being served for Grand Prix competitors.

Señor Fraga did not appear. Pedro went to the kitchen and got some coffee for the Thermos jugs and a bag of rolls. Then he returned to the room. Señor Fraga was back in bed, asleep.

He was annoyed when awakened for the third time. "Listen, my boy," he said, "you went to sleep last night when your head hit the pillow. I was awake until midnight. I had an attack of insomnia last night. Too much coffee."

"That's too bad," said Pedro. He took a sweater out of his suitcase and snapped it shut. Insomnia? Caused by coffee? Also, perhaps, by certain other beverages, lack of exercise, and a general indifference to physical conditioning.

Rosendo was up and out of bed now, and dressing. "Do I have time for breakfast, Pedro?"

Pedro looked at his watch. "For a roll and a cup of coffee—yes."

"That's all I need," said Rosendo.

"I'll pack your suitcase," said Pedro.

"Gracias." Rosendo took a sweater from it, pulled it on, and put his leather jacket on over it. *"Vamos!"*

One would think, thought Pedro, that Señor Fraga was leading the team. Rosendo led it, Pedro knew, only when he was behind the wheel of Car 25. Otherwise he was not a leader.

And what am I? Pedro asked himself, as he finished packing Señor Fraga's suitcase. I am a bellhop, a male nurse, and a valet to a temperamental character. And I thought of myself as a glamorous copilot in the Grand Prix!

157

But Pedro was excited just the same. The sun was rising over the pampas to the east, sending its bright light up into the mountains to sparkle on the snow-capped peaks to the west. The mountain air of Mendoza, stimulating at any time, was exhilarating so early in the morning. A thin mist still clung to the vineyards. All kinds of colors delighted the eyes—the beautiful bluish white of the snow, the soft white of the rising mists, the soft gray of the buildings, the red of the tile roofs. In the air hung a pungent smell of fresh coffee and smoke from wood-burning fires.

And now in the *parque cerrado* there was the wonderful roar from the engine of Car 25 and the thrilling *eeee* as Señor Fraga peeled rubber.

Pedro was busy with the route sheet to San Juan. As they roared along his impressions were many—apprehension as they skidded in the turns, wonder at the beautiful views, and above all the impression of speed, the noise of the engine, the rush of cold wind, the whine of the tires when the car cornered.

They raced to San Juan, skirted it, and went grinding on up into the mountains. The paved road turned to dirt and gravel and they skidded up clouds of dust and stones in the corners. The road climbed dizzily higher and higher in a series of hairpin turns. There were two curves to each turn, the inner curve that carried the car into the side of the mountain, and the outer curve that carried it out to the edge of the cliff.

As they climbed higher and higher the cliff became a precipice.

When they skidded around the outer curves, Pedro's gloved hands gripped the steel bar under the bucket seat and his heart seemed to be climbing up his throat. On his left was Señor Fraga, grim, determined. On his right was a foot or two of dirt and gravel and then nothing, terrifying nothingness. Car 25 skidded to the edge of the end of the world; its rear tires gripped, dug in, and sent the car careening into the safer inner curve. Pedro's heart started down again into his chest and his hands relaxed a little on the bar. The car made a power slide around the inner curve, then raced toward the precipice, and the whole terrifying process was repeated.

Suddenly they ground up onto a plateau and plunged into a low-hanging cloud. Mist enveloped them. Señor Fraga leaned forward, hunched over the wheel, peering into the mist like a helmsman on a fogbound ship.

Pedro felt like the lookout on the ship. In his hand he held the route sheet, the chart for this dangerous voyage. They should sound foghorns, Pedro thought, to warn each other of impending collisions. Señor Fraga cursed and reduced his speed slightly.

The mist grew gray and turned to rain. It was a cloudburst pelting the car, rolling thousands of bursting drops down the windshield with such speed and intensity that the wipers failed to keep the glass clear.

Heat from their bodies condensed on the windshield inside the car, forming a blinding mist that Pedro had to wipe continually with a rag. The noises of the rainstorm rushed along with them—the splash of the tires in puddles, the sound of the drops pelting against the windshield, the clickety-click of the inundated wipers. Señor Fraga dropped his speed another notch.

Without warning the rain turned to hail. Hailstones as big as grapes poured down on the car, hammering on the hood at a maniacal rate. An onslaught of hailstones covered the mountain road and sent rear tires lurching over patches of ice.

"Diablos!" cried Señor Fraga, and shifted down to second for more security in the mountain storm.

The hailstorm stopped as suddenly as it started. The silence was startling. Señor Fraga shifted to high and sped forward along the plateau.

Where the plateau ended waited a modest curve to the right. At the point where the curve began was a natural drain over the road; a deepened stream was running across it. Pedro saw it coming. He hesitated. Should he, the novice, give advice to Señor Fraga, the veteran?

Pedro, the pitman, knew the dangers that menaced engines when such streams were forded at excessive speeds. But his warning was tactful. He did not cry, "Watch out!" or "Slow down!" He said, "It may be deep, *señor.*"

Señor Fraga was not in the mood to heed such a

warning. He was in a tense and touchy humor brought on by several things—a poor sleep, hunger, the rain, and the hail. He refused to slacken his speed for the stream. He struck it hard and straight as if it were an enemy blocking the road ahead.

Splash! The water went up into the air like a wave and washed back over the hood. It struck the windshield in a blinding flood, and Señor Fraga and Pedro ducked instinctively. Much worse, it struck the spark plugs. They pinged, choked, sputtered, and drowned. And the engine expired with them.

"Diablos!" Señor Fraga jammed the gas pedal against the floor like an impatient teacher demanding an answer from an untutored pupil. There was no answer. *"Caray!"* Señor Fraga spun the wheel. It responded sluggishly. The car's momentum had carried it beyond the stream, but soon it came to a stop by the side of the road.

"Caramba!" Señor Fraga threw up his hands in despair.

Quickly unbuckling his seat belt, Pedro reached for what he knew was needed—a dry rag and a small bottle of alcohol. Thus armed he jumped out of the car, ran to the front, and lifted the hood. Deftly his hands dried each plug with the rag dipped in alcohol.

Meanwhile Señor Fraga climbed out, stretched, lit a cigarette, and paced up and down the mountain road.

Pedro was drying the eighth and final plug when the

roar of a racing engine heralded the arrival of another car. It was Renaldo Gracciani in Car 17.

With a glance, Gracciani took in what had happened and slackened his speed. The splash made by his car was not enough to create a crippling wave, but it did throw a certain amount of icy water on Señor Fraga. *"Diablos!"* Rosendo cursed, and shook his fist at the offender.

Señor Gracciani answered with a jaunty salute and a jocular, *"Hasta la vista."* Then he was gone, skidding around the curve and racing down toward the valley.

Rosendo shouted another epithet and waved his fist for a second time. His anger and frustration were apparently deepened by the knowledge that his own rash driving had caused the delay.

Pedro had finished drying the plugs. But he purposely stalled a moment. He figured that if Señor Fraga took the wheel in his fury he might plunge them off the mountain road and over the precipice. Pedro decided to take the cap off the distributor and check the points to see if they, too, were wet.

"Diablos!" cried Señor Fraga. "How much more work will have to be done?"

Pedro was in command of the situation and he knew it. This was the time, he felt, for a firm stand. He looked up and spoke calmly. "I didn't wet the plugs and points, Señor Fraga."

Rosendo glared. Then he growled and lit another cigarette. Finally he grunted. "All right, it was my fault. I'll admit it. I didn't realize that blasted stream was so deep. But can we hurry it up a bit, eh?"

"I think we're ready now," said Pedro, speaking of himself and the engine—the calmer and more efficient two thirds of the team.

"Bueno," said Señor Fraga, in a milder tone of voice.

They hurried into the car and Señor Fraga pressed the starter button. Pedro listened anxiously. Would it catch? The starter motor whined. The spark flashed through the dried plugs and the engine came to life with a wonderful roar.

"Bueno!" cried Rosendo. Leaning over, he gave Pedro a whack of congratulation.

Down from the mountains to the valley plunged Señor Fraga, braking heavily, shifting down constantly, wrenching through one hairpin turn after another in a desperate effort to catch the car that had passed. On every outside corner Pedro got a breath-taking view of the sheer drop on the other side of the precipice. The length of this drop diminished as they raced down the mountainside, and with it Pedro's concern. But two other worries appeared.

Señor Fraga, in desperate downhill racing, was merciless with both clutch and brake. Pedro began to wince every time Rosendo jammed on the brakes or shifted gears. Sooner or later under pressure like that the clutch would start to slip, the brakes to fade. To fix fading brakes or replace a slipping clutch—those were jobs that would take skill far superior to that required for the drying of wet spark plugs. Nor would the work be done in the comparative serenity of a garage in Buenos Aires. It would be done up in the cold, wet mountains or down in this hot and humid valley.

The contrast in climate was fantastic. They had been shivering up in the mountains; now they were sweating under their leather jackets. They loosened them and took off their gloves. Waves of moist heat rose up from newly planted fields of crops and fields of wild flowers.

The road over the floor of the valley was a dirt highway, which wound through the fields and climbed again up into the mountains to the city of La Rioja. Car 25 had spurted and skidded halfway through the valley when Rosendo Fraga caught sight of Car 17, driven by Renaldo Gracciani.

"Caray!" he cried, and put more pressure on the accelerator.

At just that moment a curve in the road made him brake and shift down. Around the corner they skidded. Rosendo was powering up out of the turn when another cloud suddenly enveloped them.

Unlike the mountain cloud, damp and cold, this was soft, fluttery, and warm. The components of this cloud were not tiny drops of moisture or big drops of rain or hail. They were butterflies, a blinding cloud of them rising off the flowers in the hot, humid fields.

"Diablos!" cried Señor Fraga. He was still putting

pressure on the gas pedal as he leaned forward, peering through the fluttering wings for glimpses of the road ahead.

Softly but relentlessly the butterflies covered the windshield, plastering it with a beautiful and blinding mosaic of multicolored wings.

"*Caramba!*" cried Señor Fraga. There were no more glimpses of the road ahead. All Señor Fraga could see were wings—green, yellow, purple. With a curse he wrenched his foot off the gas pedal and stepped on the brake.

Too late. The car skidded, struck a shallow ditch, bounced into the air, and started to overturn. As it crunched down on its right side Pedro heard a sharp report, followed by a violent thump.

The next thing he knew his face was in a clump of wild flowers and his right elbow was digging into spring mud. Señor Fraga, suspended by his seat belt, was sagging against his pitman. Car 25, its wheels still spinning, was lying on its side in a farmer's field.

Señor Fraga cursed the butterflies as he reached out and switched off the ignition. Then, still suspended in the seat belt, he asked, "Are you all right, Pedro?"

"*Sí, señor,*" said Pedro.

"*Bueno,*" said Señor Fraga. He struggled up to the side of the car and jumped to the ground. It gave way, being mud. Rosendo cursed the mud now as well as the butterflies. Then he leaned over and helped pull Pedro out.

While Señor Fraga stood in the mud maligning it and the butterflies, Pedro inspected the car, and said, "It was the right front tire that blew."

"The what?" said Señor Fraga. In his anger and frustration he had forgotten the loud report.

"The right front," said Pedro. "We've got a flat."

"Can I help?" said a strange voice.

They turned to see a small boy, wearing a large straw hat. "My father is coming," he said, and pointed at a man on horseback riding across the field.

"Good," said Señor Fraga.

The boy and his father were joined by several other farmers—strong as well as sympathetic. Their arrival brought out Señor Fraga's hearty, congenial self. Rosendo assumed command, assigning each farmer to a different part of the car, and then he cried, "All right, all together now, *amigos—uno, dos, tres!*"

They gave a mighty heave and Car 25 came up off its side. Then Pedro took over, quickly and surely. The jack sank into the mud, but the farmer's boy produced a flat board which acted as a platform.

Pedro was spinning the lugs off the wheel when Car 15 roared by with a jaunty wave from its pitman.

"*Diablos!*" cried Señor Fraga, who was distastefully cleaning the butterflies off the windshield.

Pedro was securing the lugs on the spare when the second car raced by, Number 16.

Señor Fraga glared at his competitors as they raced

down the flat valley road. Then he turned to Pedro. "Ready?"

"*Sí,*" said Pedro. "But I think we'd better push it out of the field. We won't get any traction in this mud."

"All right," said Señor Fraga. "Come on, my good friends," he called to the farmers. "Help us once more, if you please."

The farmers complied willingly, pushing, shoving, and heaving. Car 25 rolled out of the mud, across the ditch, and onto the road.

"*Muchas gracias!*" cried Señor Fraga.

Pedro shook the small boy's hand. "*Gracias,*" said Pedro, with a smile.

"*Buena suerte!*" said the boy.

Eeee, cried the protesting tires. And they were racing down the valley road again.

Pedro's thoughts raced along with the car. Señor Fraga had committed another error, which had cost them two more places in the competitive standing. For the second time the *señor's* emotions had got the better of his reasoning.

Lunging from one impulse to the next Señor Fraga celebrated too much, neglected physical conditioning, and became more vulnerable to strain and stress. Confronted by a ridiculous but nonetheless crippling obstacle, a cloud of butterflies, he became infuriated and tried to bull his way through. The result? A flat tire, a flip into a muddy field, and a serious loss of time and standing.

Pedro glanced at the object of this critical analysis. Señor Fraga was driving fast but not furiously. Apparently he had been sobered by the accident. Pedro's hopes rose. It was quite possible that Señor Fraga would see the error of his ways and match his natural skill with a certain self-discipline.

Pedro glanced at the route sheet, held in hands still muddied by the field. The *hoja de ruta* showed the road twisting through the valley and winding up into the mountains again to the city of La Rioja. Where the valley road began to climb was a mark on the map for a fuel stop. When Pedro warned Señor Fraga about the fuel stop, he nodded. Then he said something that made Pedro's pulse quicken. "Pedro, after this fuel stop, you'll drive about two thirds of the way up to La Rioja. All right?"

"Certainly, sir," said Pedro. This was what he had been waiting for—a chance at the wheel.

Meanwhile Señor Fraga was doing better. He caught up with Car 16 on a curve and passed it spurting down a short, straight stretch. And he was gaining on Car 15 when they switched seats at the fuel stop.

CHAPTER 9

As THE attendants pumped in the gas, Señor Fraga gave Pedro his driving instructions. "All I want you to do, Pedro, is to maintain your position between Cars 16 and 15. Don't try to pass Car 15, but don't let Car 16 pass you."

"*Si, señor.*" Pedro's voice was hoarse. His heart was beating fast; his hands were moist with excitement. And he was impatient with the attendants. He felt like shouting at them, Hurry up! Car 15 had disappeared on and up the mountain road. Car 16 was coming in sight to the rear. Hurry up!

He didn't have to shout. The tank was full. The attendants were crying, "Good luck!" The small crowd gathered around the fuel truck let out a cheer as Pedro stepped on the gas, snapped out the clutch, and peeled rubber.

This, thought Pedro, is the life. So much better

than fixing a flat in the field or drying spark plugs beside a mountain stream. To be copilot was far superior to the position of pitman. There was power here to command, plenty of it, and prestige, too. Those farm folk waving and cheering from the side of the road—they're cheering me, thought Pedro, not Señor Fraga, who was eating rolls and drinking coffee from the Thermos.

Pedro shifted to high—there was power to spare. But the mountain road, becoming steeper, drained some of the power, and Pedro had to shift down to second. Driving in second wasn't quite as exciting as driving in high; it was more conservative. Pedro wanted to be dashing, daring.

He was driving up through a hairpin turn on the outer curve. The car was skidding toward the right side of the road. Pedro realized that there was no fence, no guard rail, just a few boulders between them and a sheer drop off a cliff—disaster, death, perhaps. And it was his decision to make now on how close he wanted to come to catastrophe.

Pedro's right foot started to switch from accelerator to brake. In the nick of time he prevented it; braking would increase the skid. Instead Pedro forced himself to maintain pressure on the gas pedal. The rear wheels dug in and sent the car powering up and away from the edge of the cliff toward the inside curve of the hairpin turn.

A sidewise glance at Señor Fraga showed him still

munching rolls and drinking coffee. Does he have confidence in me? Pedro asked himself. Or is he just pretending to have confidence to make me feel better?

Pedro took the next two turns conservatively, "feathering" the accelerator, maintaining that delicate balance between the skid and the pull of power.

A glance in the rear-vision mirror showed no sign of Car 16. That was good. He was holding his own. But he wanted to do a little better than that. How? He couldn't take too much of a chance on the outer curves; a slip there could be disastrous. On the inside curves of the hairpins, however, the mountainside was on the left; a slight miscalculation there would not be fatal. So he decided to try more speed on the inside corner.

Skillfully negotiating the outside curve, he increased his pressure on the accelerator and raced into the *U* of the hairpin turn. His skid was now to the left, but the pull of power was to the right. It was a struggle between the two and the skid was winning out. He had destroyed the delicate balance of power. He was losing control, spinning out!

Eeee. The tires screamed a protest as the car skidded toward the jagged shelf of rock. *Whang.* With a terrible noise the tail of the car struck the rock.

"Shift down, fast!" cried Señor Fraga.

The impact of the collision was a sickening sound to Pedro. He almost lost complete control. But Car 25 was still alive, bouncing off the shelf of rock. With a jerk Pedro shifted down to first and salvaged speed. When he stepped on the gas the car responded faithfully. Roughly he shifted up to second and carefully maneuvered around the outside corner. Then, and only then, did he dare glance at Señor Fraga.

Señor Fraga was wiping off coffee that had spilled on his pants. But he was speaking with surprising tolerance. "Don't try to drive through these mountains, Pedro. Drive around them."

"*Sí, señor,*" said Pedro humbly. He had learned a lesson. Taking the wheel of the racing car on the road and feeling its speed and power had an intoxicating effect on a driver's brain. As pitman Pedro could sit back and easily criticize the man at the wheel. But when Pedro himself was at the wheel the view was different.

Pedro drove on steadily in second gear, doing what he had been told to do, maintaining his position. He realized how closely he had come to losing it; a little less luck in that collision and Car 25 could have been crippled.

Pedro had learned something else with the trained touch of his right foot and his right hand; the clutch was beginning to slip and the brakes to fade. Relentless driving had taken its toll. As a pitman Pedro resented that merciless pressure on clutch and brakes. But as copilot he could understand the driver's determination to get every ounce of speed out of the car. The more daring the driver, the heavier was his foot, and the more strain on the engine. Pedro imparted the news about the brakes and the clutch calmly, as he thought a copilot should.

Señor Fraga was not alarmed. "That's to be expected with this mountain driving, Pedro. Can we make it all right to La Rioja?"

"I think so," said Pedro.

"Good," said Señor Fraga. Consulting the route sheet, Rosendo saw the mountain road soon leveling off on a plateau. When they reached it, he said, "I'll take over now, Pedro."

Pedro nodded. He had feared that he might be fired after the tail spin into the mountainside. Fortunately, the accident had not crippled the car. Coming out of it almost unscratched, Pedro had completed the job he had been asked to do—to maintain his position and give Señor Fraga a rest of about two hours.

Eeee. Señor Fraga was at the wheel again, rested and determined. There was a straight, open stretch of road on the plateau to La Rioja and Rosendo was taking full advantage of it. The needles on the "tach" and speedometer were soaring and the roar of the engine was rising higher and higher.

Pedro was studying the route sheet. "Curve to the right in two kilometers," he said.

Señor Fraga nodded, picked a cutout point, braked, and shifted down. As he powered up out of the curve there came into sight the object of his chase, Car 15.

Quickly but smoothly Rosendo shifted to high and

173

poured on all the power the engine could provide. Car 25 raced by Car 15, getting ahead just in time for another cutout point. Rosendo put more pressure on the brakes, made a smooth shift down to second, and skillfully skidded the car through the curve.

Coming out of the turn Rosendo shifted to high, roared down a short straight stretch, and slackened his speed; they were in the outskirts of La Rioja. The second lap was about to end.

But the second lap was not over for Pedro. There was much work to be done in the pit. He planned to change the clutch and brakes, rather than adjust them. He figured that a job such as this would take him most of the next morning.

At first Pedro had resented the *parque cerrado* and the rules that locked the car in the park and allowed work on it only on the driver's day off. Now he saw sense in the procedure. He was tired after the long day's run from Mendoza. Yet he felt much more satisfied than at the end of the first lap. He had accomplished much more. He could, he felt, eat dinner and go to bed with his mind at rest. In the morning he would wake up refreshed for work on the clutch and brakes. In the afternoon he would exercise. The following morning he and the car would be ready for the next lap from La Rioja to Tucumán.

As for Señor Fraga, he had no need to worry. With Pedro's help he had regained almost all the ground he had lost. And he would profit from his mistakes. Surely he would see that his lack of physical conditioning had adversely affected his driving.

Señor Fraga seemed subdued. But he perked up somewhat as car-dealer friends came up and gathered around, shaking hands and offering congratulations. They, Pedro knew, hadn't seen the mistakes made at the mountain stream and in the cloud of butterflies.

Señor Fraga became cheerful and congenial. He accepted an invitation to dinner for himself and his pitman-copilot. But he did not become boisterous or boastful. He smoked very little and confined himself to a moderate amount of beer. He declined an invitation to a *confitería*. He was going to bed; the playboy from Buenos Aires was going to behave himself.

They were staying in La Rioja at the Hotel Provincial, an almost exact replica of the hotel at Mendoza. On returning to the hotel Señor Fraga received a telegram. It was from Maria in Buenos Aires. She was going to meet him in Tucumán.

Señor Fraga was delighted. Pedro was alarmed. The situation was complicated enough without women.

"Tucumán!" cried Señor Fraga, waving the telegram. "Warm, romantic, the flower garden of the republic! Tucumán the beautiful! Maria the beautiful! *Caramba!*"

Pedro said nothing.

Señor Fraga noticed the silence. "You're not afraid of women, are you, Pedro?"

"Certainly not," said Pedro indignantly. He wasn't afraid of them. It wasn't that. It was a question of complications. Pedro had to think of the car, the engine, and Señor Fraga's temperament. That was enough.

Señor Fraga laughed and thumped Pedro on the back. "Someday, Pedro, you will fall in love. Then everything will change."

"Perhaps," said Pedro. He doubted it very much.

They got into their beds, put out the lights, and went to sleep. It was early. Señor Fraga snored.

Something woke Pedro up. Señor Fraga had stopped snoring. He was reading by a night light near his bed.

"Does this light bother you, Pedro?"

"No, *señor*," said Pedro. It was too bad Señor Fraga was not a better sleeper. He needed exercise in fresh air. Was he too old for it? He was thirty-two, perhaps thirty-three. That was a lot older than nineteen. But in the ever-increasing group that played soccer were men even older. Did Señor Fraga really have a bad knee from polo? Which knee?

Pedro drifted off to sleep. He woke up again. Señor Fraga's bedside light was out, but the *señor* was not snoring. Pedro's eyes adjusted to the darkness, but could discern no shadowy bulk in the *señor's* bed. Pedro turned on his own bedside light and investigated. Señor Fraga had departed. Where had he gone? Pedro was afraid he knew where—to the bright lights and cheerful company of a *confitería*.

Pedro was unhappy; he was annoyed. Señor Fraga's nocturnal habits were jeopardizing the success of Car 25. The car was giving its all, all its polenta. The pitman, and copilot, was trying to do the same. But the driver was letting them down by continuing to be a playboy. It wasn't fair.

But what, Pedro asked himself, can I do about it? Señor Fraga is a veteran; I am a novice. He owns the car and has financed our participation in this Grand Prix. I can't reform this playboy; he'll have to reform himself.

Pedro rose early and left for breakfast and work. He was disturbed and annoyed, for Señor Fraga had come in late from the *confitería,* plopped into bed, and snored through what was left of the night. Work on the engine, though, restored Pedro's equanimity. Using open-end wrenches and socket wrenches he had put in a new clutch in two hours' time. Then, adding a screw driver and pliers to his mechanical equipment, he had done about an hour's work on the brakes, changing the whole shoe in the front set.

Feeling much better with work well done, Pedro confirmed his soccer game with the Hunters and then returned to the Hotel Provincial for lunch.

Señor Fraga was getting up, his face black with beard, his eyes puffy, and his jaws slack. The aspirin bottle was open. "I have a sinus headache," he said. "It's this mountain air."

"Too bad," said Pedro. "Will you join me for lunch?"

Rosendo frowned. "Is it that late?" He yawned. "I don't feel very hungry," he said, "but I will join you nevertheless."

For lunch Pedro ordered what had become his favorite dish, *bife a caballo*. Señor Fraga had fruit, coffee, and toast. He looked a little better, because he had shaved. Now he felt a little better. He sipped his coffee and smiled. "I'll let you in on a little secret, Pedro. I couldn't sleep, so I got up and went out last night. I met some old friends in the *confitería*." Señor Fraga chuckled. "One story led to another, and before I knew it the hour was late."

"Too late," said Pedro, before he could stop himself.

"What did you say?" said Señor Fraga coldly.

"I said, 'Too late.' I mean the race we're in." Pedro was having trouble matching his thoughts to words.

"What about the race we're in?" snapped Señor Fraga.

"It's quite a strain," said Pedro. He was sorry that he had started this conversation, but he was stuck with it.

"You're feeling the strain, eh?" said Señor Fraga.

"No, *señor,*" said Pedro, his face reddening. "I am not feeling the strain. I am getting plenty of sleep."

"What you mean then," said Señor Fraga coldly, "is that I'm feeling it. Is that what you mean?"

Pedro sighed. He had to say it. "*Sí, señor,*" he said sadly. "That is what I mean in a way." He frowned.

"I mean that a contest like this requires training just like soccer or boxing."

"Humph," said Señor Fraga. "And you don't think I'm training, eh? Is that it?"

"I'm afraid that is what I think," said Pedro, as quietly as possible.

"Very well," said Señor Fraga. He turned, summoned the waiter, and paid the check.

Pedro sat there on pins and needles. He, the naïve novice, had dared to criticize the temperamental veteran. He had a feeling that he was going to be fired in the dining room of the Hotel Provincial at La Rioja.

Señor Fraga was counting out a tip, a generous one, as usual. "I must remind you, Pedro," he said in a haughty tone, "that I am the captain of this team as well as the owner of the car and the financier who pays the bills. As captain, owner, and financier, Pedro, I can say only this—if you don't like the way I'm running this team you can resign and I will pay your bus or plane fare back to Buenos Aires. Agreed?" He gave Pedro a cold and critical look.

Pedro swallowed. "Agreed," he said.

Señor Fraga got up and left the table. "Think it over this afternoon, Pedro. I'll be up in the room. I'm going to take a siesta."

"*Sí, señor,*" said Pedro.

Pedro thought it over. He didn't want to resign. He wanted Señor Fraga, the playboy from Buenos Aires,

179

to reform. And that apparently was too much to expect. As a matter of fact, the schedule was almost perfectly suited to Señor Fraga's pattern of conduct. A day of hard, fast driving would be followed by a celebration in a *confitería* with the local car dealers. The next day Señor Fraga could recuperate. The following day he would be ready to race again. How ready? That was Pedro's point. He was convinced that if Rosendo really trained, he would greatly improve his standing in the Grand Prix. It was sad for Pedro to see someone with great ability limit his potential by poor physical conditioning.

Pedro was depressed as he set out for his soccer game. He wondered if he should resign and decided to defer his decision until dinnertime. Meanwhile he would try to forget his worries by exercising.

He felt better after the game. His spirits lifted. He would not resign; he couldn't quit. He said as much to Señor Fraga.

"Very well, Pedro," said Rosendo coolly. He was aloof. His attitude indicated that he had been insulted. But he was going to let bygones be bygones.

Rosendo announced that he was having dinner with some friends, but he added coldly that he would be in early—they would go over the route sheet together for the next day's run to Tucumán.

Pedro had dinner with the Hunters. The soccer game was discussed, and Pablo Hunter asked why Señor Fraga never joined in.

"He has a trick knee from an old polo injury," said Pedro.

Juan Hunter raised his eyebrows. "Polo?" he said. "When did Rosendo ever play polo?"

"I don't know," said Pedro. It really didn't matter. Señor Fraga didn't have to lie about it. But perhaps that was all part of the pattern.

Dinner over, they strolled in the plaza. Pretty girls smiled, small boys asked for autographs. From a *confitería* came the sound of a small orchestra playing a tango. It was very pleasant, but Pedro remembered how early he had to get up for the next day's run. There was also that conference with Señor Fraga over the route sheet.

Pedro said good night and went up to his room. Señor Fraga was not in. Pedro undressed and got into bed. Nine o'clock. Nine-thirty. Still no sign of Señor Fraga. Pedro was healthily tired. He dropped off to sleep.

Pedro woke up. A door closed; the bathroom light went on. Pedro glanced at his watch—eleven o'clock. It was not excessively late, but take-off time was at six A.M., which meant getting up at least by five-thirty. If Señor Fraga were lucky he would get about six hours of sleep. It was not enough. Moreover, he and Pedro had not gone over the route sheet together. The team was not being run efficiently. There was top performance under the hood, but something less than that behind the wheel.

But what can I do about it? Pedro asked himself.

Señor Fraga had been careful to point out his points of control; he was the owner of the car and the financier of the trip. Señor Fraga held almost all the cards; it was up to him to play them properly.

Tires were screaming, engines roaring. The starter's flag was dipping in the plaza of La Rioja. Señor Fraga was snatching his breakfast behind the wheel. Slow in getting out of bed, he had missed it again, but Pedro had filled the Thermos jugs with coffee and procured a bag of rolls.

Pedro was satisfied with his work on the car. The new clutch worked well; the brakes were fine. But in what kind of shape was Rosendo Fraga? He was grumpy. He was annoyed at himself for oversleeping and missing breakfast. He was annoyed at the weather, which was cold and damp. Señor Fraga shivered and handed the empty Thermos cup to Pedro. "It looks like rain," he growled, and he tucked his silk scarf tighter around the neck of his leather jacket.

"I'll be glad to get out of these blasted mountains," he added.

Pedro nodded. So would he. At first the snow-peaked mountains had seemed beautiful. Gradually, grindingly, they had become just so many obstacles, dangerous and treacherous. The hairpin curves took Pedro's breath away as they revealed sheer drops into space. The constant swerving from left to right made him dizzy. Yes, he too would be glad to get out of these blasted mountains.

The starter's flag was raised for Car 25. Rosendo was stabbing grimly at the accelerator. The flag dropped. Rosendo stepped on the gas, snapped out the clutch, peeled rubber, and sent Car 25 rocketing out of La Rioja.

Up over the plateau they roared and into the mountains. Clouds closed in on them, cutting off visibility. Señor Fraga snarled and growled and braked and stepped on the gas again. Stones, spun out by the screeching tires, ricocheted off the mountainside and pinged against the car. The two tires on the right, on the edge of the precipice, dug down through loose gravel, found traction, and hurled the car forward out of danger—for the moment.

A gray cloud, which hung over them like a sagging canopy, gave way and drenched them with rain. The rain turned to hail, and stones of ice drummed on the top and hood. Hunched over the wheel, Señor Fraga drove on grimly, braking, shifting, and accelerating.

Anxiously Pedro watched the gauges. Water temperature going up—too high, boiling over! Quickly Pedro reached for the pump that changed the water. As he pumped the cooler water into the radiator and expelled the boiling water onto the road, a sharp pressure on the brakes and a lurch to the left wrenched the pump out of his hands.

Recovering his balance, he peered through the hail

183

and saw a car crumpled against the mountainside on the inside curve. He was just able to catch its number, thirteen, before Señor Fraga spurted by, muttering to himself, "Thirteen—unlucky—too bad."

Pedro resumed pumping. The mercury in the temperature gauge was sinking satisfactorily. Suddenly the whine of the tires and the roar of the engine sounded louder—the hailstorm had stopped. The improved visibility showed a short, straight stretch of level road. Señor Fraga greeted it with a burst of power.

The short stretch led to a curve to the right. Señor Fraga picked his cutout point, braked, and skidded around the curve. By the side of the road, stopped on a rock shelf, was Car 14, its crew frantically working on it.

Señor Fraga hardly gave them a glance. The mountain road was beginning to wind down to the plains. Señor Fraga was braking, shifting down, skidding through one curve after another, down, down, down, with each view from the outside curve clearer and closer to the country below.

The sun came out and it began to get hot. The lower they drove, the more intense grew the heat. It moved in on them, close and humid, as they reached the floor of the valley and began racing through flowery fields.

Pedro glanced at Señor Fraga. His face was a study in stress. The strain of the demanding mountain driving was showing plainly in the lines around his eyes and mouth. Yet he had done well. Helped by the new clutch and brakes, he had brought Car 25 rapidly over a dangerous stretch of road.

Cars 13 and 14 had been left in the lurch. Car 17 with Renaldo Gracciani and Car 12 with Tomas Schmidt were still ahead, but probably not so far ahead. They could be caught, perhaps, before they reached the town of Catamarca on the road to Tucumán.

Señor Fraga was literally sweating it out. Big drops of perspiration were rolling out from under his crash helmet, running down along his nose, and dripping into his mustache. Sometimes they tickled and Señor Fraga swiped at them when he got one hand free.

"Caray!" He swiped hard and smacked himself in the face. *"Diablos!"* cried Señor Fraga in pain, dismay, and alarm. "Bees! I'm stung!"

Bees! They had flown in from the flowers in the field. The pain in Señor Fraga's sweat-stained cheek snapped his taut nerves. Car 25 skidded out of control, spun out, struck a boulder by the side of the road with a terrible bang, bounced over a ditch, and ground to a stop in the field.

Cursing, Señor Fraga switched off the ignition, scrambled out of his seat belt, and fled from the car, running this way and that like a man out of his mind.

Pedro brushed off a bee, ducked away from another, and got out of the car. There was mud in the field. Remembering a lecture from his first-aid course, Pedro scooped up a handful of mud and pursued his frantic captain. "Here, Señor Fraga!" he called. "Put this on your face!"

Señor Fraga pulled up short and Pedro, coming upon him suddenly, applied first aid so abruptly that he covered at least half of Rosendo's tortured physiognomy with the moist soil of Argentina.

"*Diablos!*" cried Rosendo.

Pedro apologized. "I didn't mean to apply it so firmly, Señor Fraga, but you stopped so suddenly—"

"*No importa!*" cried Señor Fraga. "It doesn't matter. It feels better. Thank you."

"It's too bad," said Pedro. "When you need more mud, *señor,* just tell me. There is plenty more where that came from."

"That blasted bee!" cried Rosendo. "The cursed bite is swelling. By tonight it will be the size of an egg. What will Maria think?"

"I don't know," said Pedro. Nor did he care. He was concerned with the time they had lost. A bee sting was painful, but Señor Fraga should put up with it and get on with the race. Pedro had an idea.

"Suppose I drive for a while, *señor?* Then you can hold a fresh pack of mud against the bite."

"A good idea," said Señor Fraga.

Pedro scooped up some fresher mud and put a new dressing on Señor Fraga's wound. They got in the car. The rear wheels skidded, but Pedro did not panic and put too much pressure on the gas pedal. With steady pressure and quick shifting, he skidded and bounced the car back on the road and stepped on the gas.

As they raced away Pedro's spirits lifted. The car was still performing well. And that was what mattered most. If Señor Fraga wouldn't condition himself physically it was just too bad. He would wear himself down in mountain driving. His nervous tension would increase and when a bee stung him he would blow up and lose control. It was too bad. If Señor Fraga could keep in shape they would do very well in this race. But it was apparent by now that Rosendo would not submit to self-discipline. The best thing to do, Pedro thought, was to look on the bright side of the Grand Prix. When Señor Fraga got tense and tired, that gave Pedro a chance at the wheel. And he loved to drive.

He loved the roar of the engine, the rush of the wind, the sensation of power that the racing car gave him. He liked the feeling that he could drive as fast as he wished—how often could a teen-ager do that? He liked the occasional cheers from bystanders, the friendly waves of hands.

He was driving better. He was sure of that. He always had confidence in the car; what he had lacked was confidence in himself. He was getting it. His shifting was smooth, his cornering was deft and fast. It was easier for him on the curves to steer with the accelerator, to maintain that delicate balance between a controlled drift and a spin out of control.

This corner here, for instance. He braked, shifted down, and skidded around it nicely. Beyond the corner the road forked. Left or right?

Señor Fraga was sitting in the copilot's seat, his eyes half-open, still pressing the mud pack against the bee sting.

Pedro thought he remembered the fork on the route sheet. The road to Tucumán lay to the left through the town of Catamarca.

Pedro turned to the left and roared away. Five kilometers flashed by and Pedro began to feel uneasy. Another kilometer, and he began to feel alarmed. The road was disintegrating. It had become rough and bumpy. There were holes that could not be avoided at high speed. When the front wheels hit these holes the steering wheel tried to wrench itself free. Pedro winced as the car crunched forward from one collision to the next. He felt sorry for the car. The shock absorbers were taking a beating. He reduced his speed, but his uneasiness increased.

There was no sign of other traffic. Pedro glanced at the speedometer. It showed nine kilometers since the fork in the road. Worry gnawed at him. Had he taken the wrong turn at the fork?

Señor Fraga, route sheet in hand, should have said "Left," or "Right." But Señor Fraga had been holding the mud pack against his bee sting.

Pedro saw a store coming up on the right. He decided to stop and ask directions. He braked and steered to the side of the road in front of the *almacén de ramos* —general store.

Señor Fraga emerged from his partial coma. "Why are we stopping here?"

"To ask directions," said Pedro.

Señor Fraga removed his mud pack. "To ask directions!" he cried. "Don't tell me we're lost!"

Pedro did not have time to answer. Several customers had hurried out of the store and were crowding around the car. They were all admirers, and Señor Fraga had to respond to admiration. Removing his mud and tidying up his face with a handkerchief, he exchanged congenial greetings with one and all.

The proprietor of the store emerged, a short, stout man with a mustache much larger and bushier than Señor Fraga's. A cigar under the mustache gave off puffs of strong-smelling tobacco. Beads of perspiration glistened on the well-filled face. "What can I do for you, gentlemen?" he asked. "Refreshments of some kind? Drinks? Crackers? Cheese?"

"The road to Catamarca, *señor?*" said Pedro, anxiously. "Is this it?"

"Oh no, *señores!* The road to Catamarca is back there." A stout arm waved. "Go back to the fork in the road and take the other turn."

Señor Fraga growled. "Why didn't you take the other turn, Pedro?"

Pedro was hot and somewhat irritable himself. "You

were supposed to be using the route sheet, Señor Fraga," he answered.

Señor Fraga scowled. He started to say something, then checked himself, remembering that he was performing in front of an audience.

The stout proprietor was pointing to Señor Fraga's face. "What's wrong, *señor?*" he asked.

"Bee sting," said Rosendo. He shrugged his shoulders bravely. "It's nothing," he said.

"A bee sting!" cried the proprietor. "Very painful. I have just the thing for it."

Señor Fraga smiled. "You are very kind, *señor,* but we really don't have time."

"It won't take a minute," said the proprietor. He scurried into the store and came back with a wad of cotton and a small bottle of yellow fluid. Opening the bottle, he quickly soaked the cotton. "Good for all bites!" he cried. "Soothing! Takes out the pain, reduces the swelling!"

"You are very kind," said Señor Fraga. He bathed his bee sting, sighed, and said, "It does feel better. How much do I owe you, *señor?*"

"Nothing!" cried the stout proprietor. "Absolutely nothing. My contribution to the Grand Prix."

"Bravo!" cried several members of the small crowd. "*Viva* Señor Amalfi!"

Señor Amalifi beamed.

"We've got to get going," said Señor Fraga. He

handed the bottle and the cotton to Pedro. "Take these. I'm going to drive."

Pedro checked a sudden impulse to throw the bottle and the cotton in Señor Fraga's face. *El gran* charlatan— the big fake, thought Pedro. How dare he imply that his copilot got Car 25 into this mess! The nerve of him! For the first time Pedro deeply resented all of Señor Fraga's histrionics, his playing to the audience —any audience—even this small group of country folk in front of the *almacén de ramos*.

Señor Fraga bathed his face again as he changed seats with his copilot. Then he waved a gallant good-by to the group. The engine was roaring as Señor Fraga jabbed at the accelerator. The crowd was standing back awed and wide-eyed.

Pedro knew what was coming and braced himself in his seat.

Eeee. The crowd cheered.

"Not so fast, *señor*," warned Pedro. "This road is full of holes."

"I'm driving now," snapped Señor Fraga.

He was indeed. Señor Fraga was attacking the bumps the way he had once attacked the railroad tracks. They were flying from one bump to the next, and the sounds coming from the abused shock absorbers were like cries of anguish in Pedro's ears.

"The shocks, *señor!*" Pedro protested. He was referring not to the shocks of the collision, but the effect on the absorbers.

191

"To the devil with the shocks!" cried Señor Fraga, his right foot continuing to press heavily on the gas pedal.

Bump. They hit a hole. *Whump.* They flew through the humid air. *Crunch.* They landed and struck another and deeper hole with a violence that was painful to both car and occupants.

"That did it!" cried Pedro.

Señor Fraga winced and slackened his speed. Too late. Now every time they struck a hole there was a violent jar.

Señor Fraga frowned, grunted, and braked to a stop. "This blasted road!" he cried. He glared at Pedro. "Why did you get us lost on such a road?"

Pedro was in no mood for respect and obedience. "Why didn't you tell me what turn to take?"

Señor Fraga unbuckled his seat belt with trembling fingers. "Don't talk to me that way. Remember who is the novice on this team."

Pedro got out of the car. "All right, who is the novice? Who just drove so fast over a bad road that he knocked out the shocks?"

Señor Fraga got out of the car and came around to the other side. His voice was a rasp. "If you had prepared the shocks properly, they would stand up under fast driving."

"Fast driving!" cried Pedro scornfully. "Crazy driving, Señor Fraga! You were driving like a lunatic!"

Señor Fraga gasped. "A lunatic!" Rosendo's face

turned almost as red as his bee sting. He advanced, fists clenched. *"Bulonero!"* he cried.

"Charlatan!" replied Pedro.

"Charlatan!" Señor Fraga's hot temper boiled over. He charged, swinging.

Pedro's agile mind flashed back to high-school boxing. He put up his fists, side-stepped, blocked a wild blow, and sent a short, straight right to Señor Fraga's solar plexus.

Señor Fraga went down with a gasp. He collapsed like a pricked balloon, sagging into the dust by the side of the road. Immediately Pedro became sympathetic. He stepped forward. "Let me help you up, *señor.*"

Rosendo's answer was another gasp.

Pedro became alarmed. Perhaps he should give artificial respiration!

But Rosendo recovered his breath. "You're fired!" he gulped.

"All right," said Pedro. He was relieved. Señor Fraga had come back to life, at least, even if his first words were extremely unfriendly.

Breathing heavily, Señor Fraga pulled himself up to a sitting position. He spoke again, laboriously. "When we get to Tucumán I will give you the bus fare to Buenos Aires."

"All right," said Pedro. It was too bad that the team had to break up, but better a breakup than a crackup. Sufficient damage had already been done. The poor car was crippled just as if it, too, had been hit in the solar plexus. Pedro spoke sadly. "I'd better fix the shocks," he said.

Señor Fraga struggled to his feet. "Never mind," he said haughtily. "You are no longer in my employ, Pedro. The car is no longer your responsibility."

"Very well," said Pedro. He climbed back in the car—as a passenger. It felt strange, sad.

Señor Fraga got in slowly and carefully. He looked much the worse for wear. The stubble of beard was coated with dust; the dust was streaked with sweat. His face resembled a sun-baked desert, covered with scrub, with one hump of mesa land—the swollen bee sting.

Señor Fraga started up the engine and drove back over the pock-marked road at a moderate speed. *Whump. Bump. Crunch.* Even at a reduced speed the damage to the shock absorbers caused jarring collisions. Each crunch jarred air out of Señor Fraga's lungs. He went from bump to bump in a series of grunts. Finally he gave in. Speaking petulantly, he said, "This won't do, Pedro. I'm afraid I'll have to ask you to fix those shocks."

"Very well," said Pedro.

Rosendo braked the car to a stop, and said, "Inasmuch as you have already been fired, Pedro, I shall consider this work as an outside job done by a mechanic and shall pay for it accordingly."

"I shall do it for nothing," said Pedro firmly.

Señor Fraga shrugged. "If you insist," he said.

Pedro took out his jack, a small, hydraulic, three-stage jack. With it he raised the front end of the car. Then, using pliers and open-end wrenches, he got at the shocks on the right front wheel. Two of them were shot. He replaced them and went on to the left front wheel.

Rosendo Fraga sat silently in the car, smoking, frowning, and brooding.

Pedro replaced two shocks in the left front wheel and glanced at his wrist watch. Forty-five minutes had elapsed. Not bad.

Forty-five minutes of silence for Señor Fraga. Finally he spoke. "All ready?" he said, and his tone was neutral.

"All ready," said Pedro.

Silently and still at moderate speed they drove back to the fork in the road. The collisions with the holes in the highway no longer jarred painfully.

At the fork in the road Señor Fraga accelerated in the direction of Catamarca. He seemed to have recovered from the bee sting and the blow to the solar plexus. He drove well, fast but not recklessly.

The route sheet in Pedro's hands showed a fuel stop in a service station at Catamarca. When they pulled in to refuel, the attendants were cheerful and congenial. Señor Fraga did not respond. Something seemed missing. As they were leaving another car pulled up, Number 14. It was the car that had broken down in the mountains. It had been repaired and was back in the race.

And so, thought Pedro, is Car 25—in spite of the bee sting, the blow to the solar plexus, and the wrong turn at the fork in the road. There was one comforting thing about this Grand Prix. It covered so much ground and had so many different aspects that one mistake or even two or three did not automatically disqualify a car. All the competitors were continually getting into trouble.

Car 25 was still in the race. But I'm out of it, thought Pedro sadly. I've been fired. Not so long ago he had faced that fact with a feeling of relief. Now he was not so sure. He had done a great deal of work on this car; he was attached to it. He didn't like to leave it.

They drove on toward Tucumán. Señor Fraga kept the pressure on. It produced results. Coming out of a curve they caught sight of a car up ahead, Car 16, which apparently had passed them during their detour.

Señor Fraga came out of the curve fast and poured on the power. It was there, all the polenta that Pedro had added to the car. Car 25 gained on Car 16. The engine roared, the air rushed by. Car 25 passed Car 16 and kept its lead.

Pedro was delighted—the car was still in fine shape —and saddened, for it no longer mattered. In Tucumán some other pitman would take over.

CHAPTER 10

Driving from Catamarca to Tucumán Señor Fraga seemed completely recovered. But in the Grand Prix, Pedro had learned, things happen as fast as the speed of the cars.

When they raced into the outskirts of Tucumán the polenta, which had been so plentiful, suddenly seemed to evaporate into thin air. Without warning the rear wheels, which had been spinning so powerfully, suddenly lost their drive. A dry, metallic noise clicked up from the direction of the rear axle. Car number 25 was in trouble again.

Rosendo Fraga, whose moods often corresponded to the car's performance, was depressed once more. "*Caray!*" he cried. Since he knew very little about engines, he swallowed his pride and asked the pitman he had just fired what the matter was.

Pedro had been asking himself the same question

and thinking of the symptoms of the car's distress—
the sudden loss of power, the lack of drive from the
rear wheels, and the metallic sound. The car had been
under a great deal of pressure; something had to give.
He made his diagnosis cautiously. "I'll take a guess,"
he said. "I think the half shaft is broken."

Broken—a terrible word to a driver of a racing car.
Burned out was bad enough for a bearing, *dead* for a
battery. But *broken*—that was the end.

In a few revolutions of the crippled drive shaft
Señor Fraga's power and prestige passed out of his
hands. He was helpless. Car 25, so recently fast and
formidable, was barely moving.

"What shall I do?" he cried almost plaintively.

"How far is it to the control point?" Pedro consulted the route sheet. "No more than two or three
kilometers. Let's keep going as long as we can."

They limped along. Spectators, increasing in number, pointed and shouted. But they did not jeer; they
were sympathetic. Small boys ran alongside, asking,
"Qué pasa? Qué pasa?" Señor Fraga looked as if he had
been hit in the solar plexus for the second time.

Car 25 staggered through the warm, flower-lined
streets of Tucumán with the terrible metallic noise
clackety-clacking up from the rear axle. Then Car 25
groaned to a stop—there was no more drive at all from
the rear.

Señor Fraga sighed and threw up his hands. "Now
what?" he asked.

"Now," said Pedro, "we get out and push."

Señor Fraga remembered something. He spoke quietly, almost apologetically. "You don't have to, you know."

"I know," said Pedro proudly. "But I'll still do what I can for the car."

For the car. Señor Fraga nodded. "I see," he said.

They got out and pushed. A couple of spectators joined in, then half a dozen—almost anyone, young or old, who could get a hand on the car. They got going fairly fast, and Señor Fraga had to stop steering from the side and get in behind the wheel. They were all running and shouting by the time they reached the finish line in the crowded plaza.

In Tucumán they again stayed in a Hotel Provincial. Car 25 went into the *parque cerrado* and Señor Fraga went off to find his friend Maria. Pedro had dinner with the Hunters and described the end of his partnership with Señor Fraga. He was careful to omit any references that would humiliate Señor Fraga, such as his uproar over the bee or his collapse from the straight right.

"It's too bad," said Juan Hunter, "but I am not surprised. Rosendo is very temperamental. You are not the first pitman to find that out."

"Alfonso Salas," Pedro murmured.

Juan Hunter nodded. "And others before him."

"I don't want to leave him in the lurch," said Pedro. "If he can't find someone else—"

"He will," said Señor Hunter. "Rosendo has lots of friends all over Argentina. They'll come up with someone, don't worry."

But Pedro couldn't help worrying. He hated to leave Car 25. In a curious way, he didn't even want to leave Señor Fraga. Rosendo was hard to get along with at times, especially after his nocturnal excursions. But he was generous, colorful, and often congenial. And before his deteriorating physical condition caught up with him, he was a skillful and successful driver.

In bed Pedro lay awake for a while with his worries. His one consoling thought was that he didn't care what time Señor Fraga returned from the *confitería*. In the morning he rose early, had breakfast, and went to the *parque cerrado* to work on Car 25. This would be his last job on the car and he wanted it to be a good one.

Jacking up the rear end, he took the right wheel out of its housing. To do this he used an ingenious tool called a wheel puller. It was a disk with four fingers. A threaded screw went through the disk. Counterpressure exerted by the screw exercised the fingers, which opened, closed, and seized with the tenacity of a crab's claw.

Out of the differential came the broken half shaft, two and a half feet long and an eighth of an inch in diameter. It had been assembled, Pedro noticed, with a good deal of grease to make its extraction easier. He could thank his predecessor, Alfonso Salas, for that. Fired, too, thought Pedro sadly.

"Buenos días, Pedro."

Pedro gave a start. It was a feminine voice. From where he was lying under the car he could see high-heeled shoes and sheer stockings on well-shaped calves. He came out from under the car slowly and saw Maria, prettier than ever. *"Buenos días,"* he said politely, and got to his feet.

"I'm interrupting your work," she apologized.

"That's all right," said Pedro. He felt uncomfortable. He resented Maria in a way; he admired her in another way. Suddenly his nose itched. He rubbed it quickly.

Maria smiled. "Now you have grease all over your nose, Pedro," she said. "Here, let me wipe it off." She brought forth a clean, tiny handkerchief, which smelled of perfume.

Pedro recoiled. "Oh, no," he said. "Don't use that. You'll ruin it." And he used the sleeve of his coveralls.

She smiled again. "You didn't get it off," she said. "You just spread it."

What did it matter? But it was nice of Maria to offer to sacrifice that dainty handkerchief. She was a beautiful woman. Someday, perhaps, he would fall in love with a woman like this. Señor Fraga had said so, and Pedro had considered the thought fantastic. Today he wasn't so sure. So much had taken place that he was now convinced that almost anything could happen.

Maria was talking quickly. "I won't take much of your time. I came, Pedro, because Rosendo couldn't bring himself to come."

"Why not?" said Pedro, puzzled.

"Because he couldn't swallow his pride," said Maria. "Not all of it, anyway."

"Ah," said Pedro.

Maria put her handkerchief back in her handbag and snapped it shut. Then she looked Pedro right in the eye. He felt a little weak all at once and wondered if he were hungry—it must be almost time for lunch.

She spoke firmly and clearly. "Rosendo wants to re-hire you," said Maria. "Would you consider it?"

"Well," said Pedro. He was staggered and he stalled for time. He wanted to accept immediately. But he held back, remembering Señor Fraga's playboy habits.

Maria was smiling. "Don't worry," she said. "Rosendo and I had a long talk. I know him very well, Pedro. He doesn't fool me."

"Ah," said Pedro. "Did he tell you about the fight?"

"Yes," said Maria.

"Ah," said Pedro again. "And he wasn't mad about that?"

"Not any more," said Maria.

"Oh," said Pedro. How much had Señor Fraga told about the fight? It didn't matter.

"We had a good frank talk," said Maria. "Rosendo

admitted his mistakes. He admitted being careless about his training."

"Ah," said Pedro. He frowned. "Still, he fired me."

"In a moment of anger, Pedro. He was very impressed with the way you behaved after that."

"What did I do?" said Pedro, puzzled again.

"You made the repairs on the car. You're still making them. That is real loyalty, Pedro."

Pedro said nothing.

"Well," said Maria. "What do you think? He has offered to rehire you. Do you accept?"

"I appreciate the offer," said Pedro politely. "But, well, wouldn't the same thing happen all over again?"

"It might," said Maria, "but I don't think so. We had a long talk. He promised to behave himself. If he doesn't"—Maria's eyes flashed—"we'll have a short talk."

"Oh," said Pedro. Could a woman change Señor Fraga? A woman like this, perhaps, if he were willing to change himself.

"Last night," said Maria, "Rosendo had dinner with me and my Tía Helena. Do you know what he had to drink? *Un vaso de leche!*"

"*Fantástico,*" murmured Pedro. So Señorita Maria had brought her Aunt Helen along as chaperon. Naturally. A young woman would not travel about unchaperoned. And Rosendo had drunk a glass of milk. Think of that! Maria had already worked a minor miracle. "It is almost too good to be true," said Pedro softly.

"It is true," said Maria. "I swear it."

"I did not mean to express doubt," said Pedro.

It was *fantástico* what a beautiful woman could do. There was, perhaps, something in this love business after all. If this reformation continued, Señor Fraga might even be persuaded to take part in outdoor exercise.

Maria was smiling. "You will continue as copilot and pitman, Pedro?"

"I will be glad to," said Pedro gallantly.

"Que bueno!" said Maria. "Then we shall all have lunch together. One o'clock."

"With pleasure," said Pedro.

Pedro had expected Tía Helena to be a little old lady in black. She was neither little nor old, and the dress she wore at lunch was as colorful as the flowers of Tucumán. Pedro was glad that he had taken the trouble to clean all the grease from under his fingernails and put on a clean shirt and tie.

"My, you look well, Pedro," said Maria.

Señor Fraga smiled benevolently. "I've taken good care of him."

"And he of you," said Maria.

Señor Fraga coughed and reached for his glass of milk.

"What do you do on your afternoon off, Pedro?" asked Tía Helena.

"We have a friendly soccer game," said Pedro.

"Does Rosendo play, too?" asked Aunt Helen.

"No," said Pedro. "He has a bad knee from playing polo."

Maria had been saying something to Rosendo. She interrupted herself to ask, "When did you play polo, Rosendo?"

"Before I met you," said Rosendo glibly.

"I didn't even know you rode horseback," said Maria.

"A long time ago," said Rosendo. "In my carefree youth."

"Oh," said Maria. She smiled. "Well, in that case, your knee has had plenty of time to recover. I'm sure a little exercise won't hurt it, and it might do you a world of good. Sitting still in that car hour after hour must be very bad for you."

"I'm not sitting still in the car," Rosendo protested. "I'm constantly flexing my knees by pushing on the brake or the clutch. Suppose I play soccer and sprain my weak knee? It will be difficult for me to drive."

"On the contrary," said Maria. "Exercise will strengthen the knee. Why leave it weak?"

Why indeed? thought Pedro. This woman is relentless.

"Yes, Rosendo," echoed Tía Helena. "Why leave a weak knee weak?"

Señor Fraga is doomed, thought Pedro. Not one woman against him, but two.

But Señor Fraga was fighting back. "I'll tell you what, Maria. When I get back to Buenos Aires, we'll play tennis together—mixed doubles."

"I think you should start exercising now," Maria insisted. "Listen, Rosendo, you expect the engine of the car to be in the best possible shape, don't you?"

"Yes," Rosendo admitted.

"Well, then—" said Maria.

That was all she said. The subject was changed, but Rosendo had already lost the argument. That afternoon, grumbling, he joined the group on the soccer field. Up and down the field he huffed and puffed with frequent time-outs for recuperation.

That night at dinner Señor Fraga had to stifle several yawns. He retired at an early hour, after asking Pedro to wake him up at five A.M. for the race to Resistencia.

Promptly at five A.M. Pedro got Señor Fraga up. Reluctantly Rosendo dragged himself out of bed. "I ache all over," he grumbled.

But he felt better after a shower.

"How did you sleep?" asked Pedro.

"Like a sloth," said Señor Fraga. "I'm hungry. Is there time for breakfast?"

"Yes," said Pedro. For the first time, he thought.

"Good!" said Señor Fraga.

They ate breakfast in the dining room, and then

Pedro went into the kitchen to get coffee for the Thermos jugs and bread and cheese for lunch. When he returned, Señor Fraga was in fine fettle. *"Vamos!"* he cried.

The starter's flag was up for Car 25 in the flower-decked plaza of Tucumán.

Pedro's pleasure over Señor Fraga's greatly improved condition was only slightly diminished by apprehension over the new half shaft. Would it work well?

The starter's flag dipped.

Eeee. The rear wheels of Car 25 dug fiercely into the plaza. The new half shaft worked well indeed.

Señor Fraga was delighted. He was driving with more deftness and dash than ever. He caught one car coming out of a corner, passed another in a straight stretch. In the second one was Renaldo Gracciani.

Meanwhile the country was changing again from the sunny, flowery scenery of Tucumán to the shady, wooded country of the quebracho tree. As they raced along, Pedro, for the first time in the Grand Prix, had a complete feeling of confidence. He had done his work in the pit fast, surely, and well. Gone was the apprehension he had once experienced as Señor Fraga swerved, skidded, and spurted. Now Pedro could fully understand what Rosendo was doing; Pedro's reflexes and anticipation had learned to work in almost the same way. And Señor Fraga was obviously in good shape.

On they raced at a dazzling speed, power-sliding

skillfully through the short, sharp curves, drifting through the long, gradual turns. Before noon they slowed down to a brisk, but not reckless, speed and drank coffee with cheese and bread.

Lunch over, the speed shot up again and kept up. The pressure Señor Fraga maintained paid off. Early in the afternoon they finally closed in on the car that had so far eluded them, Car number 12, driven by Tomas Schmidt.

They tailed Car 12 through shady woods of quebracho, past houses with waving, cheering inhabitants. Señor Fraga was using different strategy on Tomas Schmidt. Rosendo did not try to pass. He simply kept the pressure on, a tremendous amount of it.

When Tomas Schmidt spurted, so did Rosendo Fraga. When Tomas skidded daringly, so did Rosendo. Pedro could easily imagine how Señor Schmidt felt. It was like being shadowed relentlessly. Something, thought Pedro as he clung to the bucket seat, has to give.

Something gave. Suddenly Pedro's sharp mechanical ears were startled by a strange metallic sound. For a second Pedro was alarmed. Then he located the source of the sound—the car ahead. Señor Schmidt was signaling, slowing down, and stopping. Some part of his engine had cracked under the pressure.

Señor Fraga's strategy had succeeded again. He had proved that he was just as skillful a driver as Señor

Schmidt—and that Car 25 had a stronger engine. Car 25 roared past in triumph.

Rosendo was exultant. "We did it, Pedro, you and I!"

Pedro grinned. The team was together again—or together, perhaps, for the first time.

They were approaching Resistencia when the paved road turned to dirt and cut through another area heavily wooded with quebracho trees. It had rained here recently and some of the red dirt of the road had been washed out, revealing jagged stumps of quebracho. Señor Fraga reduced his speed quickly, but not fast enough. With a violent crunch the front end of the car struck an exposed stump.

They stopped, jumped out, and stared in consternation at the damage. The sharp stump had knocked a hole in the radiator; water was running out!

Pedro was crestfallen. This accident didn't seem fair. In the others there had been a reason. But this time Señor Fraga had put his best foot forward—and fate had tripped him up.

Pedro was dismayed, because the damage was not really mechanical; it couldn't be fixed by quick and skillful work with pliers and open-end wrenches, while Señor Fraga stood by impatiently puffing on a cigarette.

But Rosendo was not standing by, smoking. He was running—Señor Fraga running—up to a farmer in front of his house!

Señor Fraga was talking fast, gesticulating. Now the

farmer was disappearing, only to return quickly, holding something that looked like a potato sack.

It was a bag made of jute. Señor Fraga lost no time in rolling it tight and stuffing it into the hole in the radiator. It made a good packing. The leak was reduced to a trickle. Meanwhile the farmer brought jugs of water, which Pedro poured into the radiator.

They were off again with a wave of thanks and farewell. As Señor Fraga carefully steered between stumps he had time to talk. "In this country, Pedro, farm folk use these jute bags for everything. I've seen them roll them up tight and make an inner tube for a flat tire out of them."

"Wonderful," said Pedro. What was wonderful—the use of the jute? In a way. But Pedro was thinking of something else—how Señor Fraga had acted in an emergency. He had used his head, which seemed to be much clearer now than ever before.

Exactly one week after leaving Buenos Aires on a Friday night, Pedro and Rosendo arrived in Resistencia in the best position Rosendo had ever attained in the Grand Prix—ninth place.

"We're in the first ten!" Rosendo exulted. "Think of it, Pedro, the first ten! *Fantástico!*"

Pedro agreed. It was *fantástico,* after all that had happened. Would Señor Fraga sneak out and celebrate? Señor Fraga drank milk, ate steak, and retired early, fatigued from the day's effort, his muscles still aching healthily from the soccer game in Tucumán.

At seven in the morning Pedro left Señor Fraga asleep and hurried to the *parque cerrado*. He got the car out and drove it to a machine shop, where he had the radiator welded. Then he went carefully over the engine to prepare it for the final lap of the Grand Prix. As he worked other pitmen came up and chatted —older, more experienced pitmen. Pedro worked on happily. Things had changed considerably. He was no longer a novice. He had proved himself. He was accepted on an equal footing with the veterans.

In the afternoon at Resistencia the usual soccer game took place. Rosendo Fraga played in it more actively, his breathing was less labored, and he showed no trace of a trick knee. After the game Pedro and Señor Fraga returned to the hotel, showered, and changed into fresh clothes. Señor Fraga yawned and stretched. "I feel well, Pedro. Those workouts do wonders."

"Fine," said Pedro. Then he couldn't resist adding, "You're sure your bad knee didn't bother you?"

Señor Fraga looked at Pedro and laughed. So did Pedro.

The dining room was crowded and noisy with boisterous car crews. Many of the drivers and the pitmen were ordering wine and beer. It was Saturday night— *fiesta* time. Señor Fraga celebrated and ordered a drink called *mate,* an aromatic beverage made from tea leaves.

211

After dinner Pedro and Señor Fraga strolled in the plaza in front of the hotel. The air was perfumed with spring, and Señor Fraga's thoughts turned to romance. "Tonight," said Rosendo, "Maria and Tía Helena will still be in Tucumán. But tomorrow they will be flying back to Buenos Aires. They are going to meet us there."

"Us?" said Pedro.

"Certainly," said Rosendo. "Tía Helena has another niece, Anita, much younger than Maria and just as pretty. Tía Helena wants you to meet Anita."

"With pleasure," said Pedro politely. Just one week ago, he was thinking, I left Buenos Aires. I was just a kid working in a garage. One week ago. It seems like a year.

They strolled around the plaza. A group of young people went by in the opposite direction singing.

"Saturday night," said Señor Fraga, smiling. "*Fiesta* time."

Pedro felt a twinge of alarm.

Señor Fraga yawned. "I feel sleepy," he said. "Let's turn in."

"All right," said Pedro, relieved.

They got up at five, ate a good breakfast, packed, walked to the *parque cerrado,* and got the car out. At precisely nine minutes after six A.M. Señor Fraga peeled rubber and raced out of Resistencia. Car 25 was the ninth car to take off.

They raced south over dry, dusty dirt roads past

huge *estancias,* ranches covered with corn and wheat and dotted with cattle. At ten-thirty they slowed down for the city of Santa Fe and had one hour in which to rest and check the engine. At eleven-thirty-nine they roared away from Santa Fe on the final lap to Buenos Aires.

They raced by more *estancias,* more fields of wheat and corn, more cattle, Shorthorns and longhorns. There were even some Brahmans, the sad-looking, smooth-skinned cattle imported from India because of their resistance to heat and the diseases of hot climates.

One of these curly-horned Brahmans with a long, sad face was waiting in the dirt road on the far side of the curve about forty-five kilometers south of Santa Fe. This Brahman had strayed from the herd.

Car 25 came skidding around the curve in a power slide. Without warning Señor Fraga had the choice of crippling the Brahman and the car or taking his chances off the road. In a split second he decided on the latter course.

The Brahman lowed, the tires screamed, and Car 25 skidded off the road, knocking down a wire fence and two fence posts. There was a pinging sound from the wire, a rending sound from the fence posts, and a sickening *crunch* as Car 25 came to a stop on its side.

Something wet and warm was running down Pedro's face. He put his hand up to his head and brought it down covered with blood. Shock and alarm tried to overwhelm him. He thrust them back with facts remembered from his first-aid class; superficial cuts on the scalp are apt to bleed freely. Fishing out his handkerchief, he pressed it against the wound and turned to his teammate, Rosendo Fraga.

Rosendo was groaning. "My arm," he said. "My shoulder."

Pedro looked and received his second shock. Rosendo's right shoulder looked sickeningly distorted. It had been wrenched from its socket—dislocated!

Again Pedro had to fight off a feeling of alarm and nausea. Once more first aid helped. Señor Fraga's shoulder was dislocated. But it could be put back in place if he, Pedro, kept his head and acted calmly and coolly. Slowly they crawled out of the car, Rosendo hanging on to his right arm and Pedro holding the handkerchief to his head wound.

A Gaucho on horseback, a leathery-looking cowboy with a black mustache, galloped up. *"Hola!"* he cried. "Look what you've done to our fence!"

Rosendo Fraga was in pain, but the complaint riled him. "Why don't you keep your blasted cattle off the road?" he snapped.

The Gaucho caught sight of the dislocated shoulder. He frowned and changed his tone. "We'd better get you an ambulance," he said. He turned to Pedro. "Look at your head, *amigo*," he said. "You need an ambulance too."

"We have no time for an ambulance," said Pedro. He had wiped away the blood and examined the wound in the rear-vision mirror. It was what he had suspected, a superficial scalp cut. Quickly he found his first-aid kit and patched up his wound with gauze and adhesive tape. Now he was ready to operate on Señor Fraga.

Pedro steeled himself against the sickening sight of the dislocated shoulder, remembering that his own appearance should show calmness and confidence. "If you'll sit down," he said to Señor Fraga, "I'll put that back in place for you."

Rosendo's dust-streaked face was pale and beady with perspiration. His voice was weak. "You're sure you know how?" he said.

"It's simple," said Pedro. "I learned how in my first-aid course."

A second Gaucho had galloped up. "Better let me ride to the phone and get an ambulance," he said.

"No, thanks," said Rosendo. "We'll lose all the ground we've gained." He sat down slowly in the field. "Go ahead, Pedro, give it the works."

Pedro stepped forward, as cool and calm as he could make himself. Gently but firmly he placed both hands on Señor Fraga's right arm, one hand high, one hand low. Then, to brace himself for the counterpressure, he gently placed his left foot on Señor Fraga's chest under the shoulder socket.

"Wait a minute!" protested Rosendo. "What are you trying to do?"

"It's for the counterpressure," said Pedro. "You know, like the fingers on the wheel puller."

"Take it easy," warned Rosendo.

"Don't worry," said Pedro. "I will." Firmly, quickly, with a rolling motion to the right, Pedro snapped the shoulder back into its socket.

"*Diablos!*" cried Señor Fraga. There was some pain in his tone, but it was almost hidden by relief and admiration. "Pedro, you should be a doctor!"

"Perhaps." Pedro smiled.

Señor Fraga rubbed his shoulder ever so gently. He looked vastly relieved. As for the Gauchos, they looked deeply impressed. Pedro turned to them. "Would you help me get the car back on its feet?"

"Certainly," they chorused.

Señor Fraga could not help much. Nor could he drive. It was up to Pedro now. Rosendo had a few words of advice for his copilot. "Thanks to you, Pedro, we've lost little ground. Nobody's passed us."

"Thanks to you, Señor Fraga," said Pedro, "we had a good lead."

"In any case," said Rosendo, "this is what I want you to do—to drive the way you know how—steadily. Don't drive to overtake; drive to maintain your position. Safety fast. All right?"

Pedro was buckling his safety belt. "*Sí, señor.*"

Rosendo smiled. "Everything considered, Pedro, we've done well enough, you and I, in position as well as elapsed time. Next year, perhaps—" He left the sentence unfinished as he turned to the Gauchos and handed them his card. "My name and address. My insurance company will pay for the damage to the fence. Many thanks for your help."

The Gauchos touched their broad-brimmed hats. Pedro backed out of the field to the road, put the car in first, and peeled rubber.

The wind began to sing again; the engine roared with all its familiar power. And Pedro was where he wanted to be, behind the wheel of a racing car.

He had earned that place. Did he then have to take Rosendo's advice, drive to maintain position? Why shouldn't he drive like Señor Fraga, flying over railroad tracks and drifting dangerously around corners— why shouldn't he drive like a Grand Prix veteran?

Pedro had learned why. There were several reasons, which he recited to himself. He was not a Grand Prix driver—not yet. Perhaps he never would be. He had done extremely well as a pitman, but he had not distinguished himself as a driver. It was entirely possible that he never would. He was competent, perhaps a little better than that, but he was several classes below drivers like Renaldo Gracciani and Tomas Schmidt.

Somewhere, not so far back, those drivers were racing along the road. Some of them would crack up in this last lap, others would have engine trouble, but some of them would come on fast toward Buenos Aires.

If Pedro, trying to drive like Señor Fraga, spun out

on a curve or cracked up against a cow, one or more of his rivals would be sure to take advantage of their second opportunity. Therefore, it was Pedro's duty as copilot not to try to be sensational, but to be his own competent self.

Señor Fraga had said, "We've done well enough, you and I." Everything considered, they had done very well indeed.

So Pedro drove fast, but not recklessly, past the *estancias*, with their fields of wheat and corn and their herds of cattle. He drove faster, but still not recklessly, on the paved roads farther to the south.

He slowed down for the outskirts of Rosario and the side streets of Pergamino. He did not gain on anyone, but no one passed him.

Hunched over the wheel, he roared into the capital of Argentina, his home city, his beloved Buenos Aires. Wildly cheering crowds lined the wide *avenidas*. His heart thumped and his blood tingled—these people, these crowds in Buenos Aires were cheering Car 25, its driver, its copilot! He skidded skillfully, but not recklessly, around a rotunda and raced down the *Avenida General Paz* to the Autodrome. As he shifted down and zoomed into the Autodrome he heard the loudest cheer of all from the great crowd waiting in the stands behind the straightaway.

Did they know who was behind the wheel of Car 25—a young mechanic named Pedro Thompson competing in his first Grand Prix? Did they know what

Pedro had gone through to receive this great honor —driving the car to the finish line in Buenos Aires? It didn't really matter to Pedro whether they knew or not. What mattered was all that had taken place, the good as well as the bad, the greatest experience he had ever had. What mattered too was that Car 25 was finishing in the first ten, out of one hundred and fifty-three competitors.

It took just a matter of seconds for these thoughts to flash through Pedro's mind. Then they were gone, fading into the wild roar of the enormous crowd and the work that still remained to be done—to drive fast and well down this familiar straightaway, to pick the right cutout point from the meter markers, and to power-slide through the S turn.

What was that? A tap on Pedro's arm. Señor Fraga was pointing to the rear-vision mirror; a competitor had come up within striking distance!

"*Vaya!*" cried Señor Fraga. Go!

"*Si, señor,*" said Pedro, and he pressed harder on the accelerator.

The engine answered with a wonderful roar, a surge of thrilling power. Car 25 barreled down the straight-away. A sign flashed by on the right—*300 meters.* Pedro kept the power on. The second warning came into sight—*200 meters.* Pedro's heart was pounding and his hands were moist. The 100-meter sign appeared. Now! He cut the power, braked, and shifted smoothly down to second. He could hear the tires begin to scream, the gears to whine. He was steering skillfully into the S curve, skidding, steering with the accelerator, feathering it daringly and delicately, holding that balance between the soft skid that saves distance and the hard skid that means loss of control. Deftly he was turning the wheel now, reversing directions for the second part of the S turn.

"*Bueno!*" cried Señor Fraga. "You're holding your own!"

Holding his own! Now, coming out of the S turn into the last straight stretch, he could do better than hold his own. He could ask the engine of Car 25 for all of its power, every cubic centimeter of additional polenta that he had built into the engine.

He asked for it with firm pressure on the gas pedal. He got it with a wild and wonderful thrust of power from all the modifications, back to the rear wheels and forward again.

"You're pulling away, Pedro!" cried Rosendo Fraga.

Up over the roar of the engine rose the cheer from the huge crowd to greet the winner of this particular race at the finish line—Pedro Thompson, driving Car 25, finishing ninth in his first appearance in the Grand Prix of Argentina.

He slowed down, braked, and steered the car to its pit stop in the Autodrome—the same Autodrome where he had practiced just a few weeks ago. Now it was a frantic and fantastic place throbbing with thousands of spectators, crawling with officials who were running up, calling out, shaking hands. Who's that behind the wheel? It's Car 25, but it isn't Rosendo Fraga.

Pedro was in a blissful daze. It couldn't be the same Autodrome. And all that had happened couldn't have taken place in so short a time, even if over so great a distance.

A photographer was importuning, a reporter was scribbling. And Rosendo Fraga was wincing, but smiling, as he said, "Do you mind shaking hands gently— my shoulder. I told you who the driver was—my copilot Pedro Thompson. Yes, it's his first Grand Prix. How did he perform? Like a veteran."

The phrase rang clear through the blur of noise. "Like a veteran." Those words made all the irksome hazards fade away. Next year, far stronger, they would enter the race again, and someday they would win it, this, the greatest road race in the world.